DOCTORS IN SHADOW

When Nurse Emma Reade comes to look after Dr
Simon Conway's mother and help in his practice,
she realises it will be impossible to live in the same
house with such a man and not fall in love. But
one of the other doctors, Odile Craig, adores him
and is fiercely possessive . . .

DOCTORS IN SHADOW

BY

SONIA DEANE

MILLS & BOON LIMITED
London · Sydney · Toronto

First published in Great Britain 1981
by Mills & Boon Limited,
15-16 Brook's Mews,
London W1A 1DR

© Sonia Deane 1981

Australian copyright 1981
Philippine copyright 1981

ISBN 0 263 73705 5

Set in Monophoto Baskerville 11 on 12 pt.

*Made and printed in Great Britain by
Richard Clay (The Chaucer Press) Ltd.,
Bungay, Suffolk*

CHAPTER ONE

'AND you are Emma!'

She replied softly, 'Yes, Dr Conway.'

His voice was deep, resonant, yet firm, as he corrected, 'I'm *Simon*! Or have you forgotten our fleeting encounters?'

The words hung between them as they looked into each other's eyes with an expression of discovery.

'No; I hadn't forgotten. The last time was when I was nearly eighteen, and about to start training at the Royal Hospital ... you were just taking over the practice here, in Winchcombe.'

'Yes ... my uncle had died.' He paused for a second, 'And now you've got your S.R.N.'

Emma felt excited, bewildered, and a little afraid. There was something powerful, inescapable, about Simon Conway. A mesmeric quality which, she felt instinctively, would be difficult to resist. Added to that, he was handsome and had the air of one accustomed to being obeyed. She liked his clean-cut features; level brows and broad forehead, which swept back to a smooth well-shaped hair-line. She had thought of him vaguely during the past years, particularly since his parents and her own had always been friends, although meeting infrequently, because her father's engineering projects took him abroad for long periods.

As if reading her thoughts, Simon hastened, 'And

now your parents have gone to Kenya for a year. You must be missing them.'

'Yes,' she admitted, 'but being able to come here to look after your mother, and help in the practice—to feel that I belong somewhere—makes all the difference. It was very kind of you to invite me to stay, even had I not wished to do private nursing.'

'Family friendships are very important,' he commented. 'And quite apart from that angle, you will be invaluable, I assure you. We need someone who can take blood pressure and look after routine matters before we actually see some of the patients. It will save an enormous amount of their time, and ours. But of course, we shall have to see how my mother progresses, as to how much time you can spare us.'

Again they looked at each other with appraisal. In turn, Simon asked himself why he had not taken Emma more seriously. Now she stood before him—a challenge. She was, he realised, beautiful, with dark lustrous eyes and hair the colour of gold leaves tinting to sorrel. He could see the thick fringe of her eyelashes as she lowered her gaze, and felt a quickening of his senses.

'To be needed is essential,' she murmured. 'It gives life a purpose.'

They were standing beside her car in the drive of the Conway house—Hunter's Close—with its single-span roof, gables at both ends and dormers over the windows. It was large, and had been bought by Simon's uncle, Edward Conway, who had converted it to practice needs by additions, instead of marring the main structure. Simon had inherited the property, and now shared it with his mother, Verity, who suffered from multiple sclerosis. She had sold the original family house after the death of Simon's father, two years previously. Now, even with remissions, she needed help to combat her physical disabilities.

Emma had never been to Hunter's Close before, and looked around her with appreciation. A walled-in garden enclosed the ground on which the house stood, and was filled with the scent of June roses. In the near distance Emma glimpsed an orchard. Lavender bushes adorned a flagged pathway which strayed away into adjacent woodland. There was a feeling of stability and permanence about it all, which appealed to her, and her heart quickened its beat in excitement and anticipation.

'I think,' Simon said, 'we'd better go in; I can see my mother in the hall.'

'Oh!' Emma suddenly felt that she was in a bumpy lift. She knew Verity Conway only as her parents' friend. Would there be a great change in her? What would she be like to nurse? Live with?

Verity moved towards them stiffly, using a walking-stick.

'Emma!' she cried, 'it's good to see you.' She shot Simon a significant glance. 'We were both a little worried in case you might decide not to come. Oh, not that you wouldn't regard this as home while Hugh and Clare are in Kenya, but that you might have last-minute qualms about leaving hospital life.'

Emma laughed. 'The idea of either living in the nurses' home, or sharing a flat with friends, since our house is let furnished for a year ...' Emma made an appealing little gesture, 'I'm really quite an Orphan Annie at the moment. This is a wonderful opportunity.' She studied Verity closely, noticing how she dragged one leg as she moved about the square oak-panelled hall. And all the time, Emma was aware of Simon's presence, of the way he drew her gaze to his, emotion rushing up between them.

'This evening,' Simon said, 'you shall meet everyone in the practice. I thought it would be a good way of breaking the ice—in a glass!' he added, with an easy smile. 'We're a friendly crowd.'

Verity gave a little laugh. 'Because they're all very efficient!'

'If one tolerates inefficiency, that is all one will ever get,' he retorted good-naturedly. But the moral was there. Simon was a fair and just man, but expected his colleagues, and those employed by him, to be both responsible and proficient.

It was a hot day and Verity exclaimed, 'How about tea?' She looked at Emma. 'After driving from London . . .'

'*Please*.' Emma stopped a little shyly. How did one behave on becoming a nurse to someone previously treated with familiarity? Verity had never wanted to be called Mrs Conway, and Christian names had always been used.

'Then Simon will show you your room, and I'll ask Mrs Jessop to bring us tea on the veranda . . . Jessop will see to your cases.'

Emma looked instinctively towards her car which stood in the shade of a large beech tree immediately outside the front door.

'I'll just get my hand-case,' she murmured, darting out and taking it from the front passenger seat, grinning as she rejoined them, 'and there's no Sister to say severely, "Nurse Reade, we do not *run*!".' She paused, conscious of Verity's stiff leg and feeling a pang of guilt. Verity, she thought, suddenly and sadly, had aged, and her once pink-and-white skin had lost its bloom, while her eyes were dark-rimmed and haunting, instead of sparkling as they used to be. Again Emma felt a sensation of guilt. Her thoughts and consciousness had embraced only Simon, as though he had taken her by storm, the awareness of his presence thrilling her, the possibility of working for him, living in close proximity, awakening an intoxicating happiness .... She dragged her thoughts back to the moment. Verity would be in her early fifties. She had retained her good figure, but stooped slightly, a fact which gave her a somewhat helpless appeal.

'This is such a wonderful house,' Emma said as she moved with Simon towards the wide staircase, which curved to the right and swept up to a spacious landing. Copper jugs, filled with gladioli, flowering shrubs and delphiniums, stood against the dark panelling, bringing the scene to life. A vast staircase window allowed the sun to pour in and illuminate the scene.

'I always did like it,' Simon admitted, 'even when I was a small boy and came here for holidays.' He looked back at his mother. '*I* can snatch a cup of tea, too,' he murmured.

Upstairs, Simon opened the door of what turned out to be a small suite.

'Mother wants you to have this,' he said. 'It was

hers before she found the stairs trying. There is a bathroom and,' he opened another door, 'a small dressing room. We converted a similar suite, but with a sitting room, on the ground floor, so that Mother can get away from everything, and everyone, if she wishes.'

Emma looked at him and wondered just how he felt about sharing his house in this way; what tensions, and secrets, those four walls concealed. That he was deeply saddened by Verity's condition could be taken for granted, and on the surface he appeared cheerful and completely in control.

'If there's anything you require—anything at all—you've only to ask.'

'It looks perfect,' she said immediately, taking in the beauty of the surroundings. It was a large, cream-and-rose room, with two sets of windows, now wide open.

Simon noticed her obvious pleasure and appreciation.

'Before you really talk to my mother,' he began quietly, 'I think you should understand that, until now, she has resisted any kind of nursing help. It is only because she knows you, and I've convinced her how useful you could be in the practice, that she agreed to your coming. Oh,' he hurried on, 'she was the first to suggest your *staying* here, when she knew Hugh and Clare were going to Kenya. Please don't let there be any misunderstanding on that score.'

Emma said, 'I understand. Multiple sclerosis is not an easy disease to assess.' She thought, as she spoke, of its vagaries. It was a disease which attacked the central nervous system, affecting limbs and, often, sight. There was no possible prognosis, and remissions occurred, during which time the patient might recover sufficiently to lead a normal life. Emma, however, knew that Verity had been incapacitated for some few years, and that her condition was worsening—the fact that she was now living on the ground floor being self-explanatory. Emma added reassuringly, 'I shall allow for her feelings in every respect.'

Simon nodded his gratitude. 'She gets very impatient with herself; with her inability to do the things she wants to do. As you well know, she was very energetic before all this happened.'

'That's why, now, she needs to be helped to help *herself*, and certainly not treated like an invalid.'

'That's precisely it,' he agreed. 'Your cheerful company will make all the difference. One of her greatest blows is not being able to drive her car . . . and, obviously, I'm not available to take her out as I would like. Jessop drives, but she has days when he is not wholly in favour! With you here . . .' His smile broadened. 'It seems that I'm already mortgaging all your time!'

'Which delights me.'

There was a sudden silence. He moved towards the open door, and holding her gaze for an imperceptible second, said swiftly, 'Join us when you're ready.' The door closed behind him.

Emma stood transfixed, emotion overwhelming her. She was *here* in this lovely old house, surrounded by breathtakingly beautiful countryside that held all the magic of England. It was the beginning of adventure.

A knock came at the door, and Jessop brought in her cases. Both he and his wife were relieved that Nurse Reade was joining the household, and his rugged, mahogany-shaded face betrayed a degree of approval.

Emma smiled, said that she would like the cases put in the dressing room, commented on the beauty of the day, adding pleasantly, 'And you're Jessop?'

'Yes, Nurse.' He decided that Nurse Reade would 'do', and wasn't some jumped up bit of a girl who would take over the place if given half a chance. He left noiselessly, his white-jacketed figure suggestive of a quiet efficiency which was part of his job. He liked working for 'the doctor' and being Jack of all Trades.

Verity's first words when she saw Emma a few minutes later were, 'What an attractive gown ... not a uniform, nor a dress; and that heavenly blue suits you perfectly. I don't want uniforms around here, thank you,' she added emphatically.

Emma had chosen the gown with care. It had a yoke and was piped with white, succeeding in being neither frivolous, nor dowdy.

'I'm glad,' she said.

'It will do well for the practice, too,' Simon exclaimed. 'We like to avoid any hospital atmosphere.'

'I bought the last three outfits left in the shop,' Emma announced. That, she told herself with relief, solved the problem of clothes.

Simon looked at her very levelly, 'But we don't want any official garb at the end of the day. We try to make dinner at eight festive, as well as functional—patients allowing, of course. If one doesn't aim for a specific time, life becomes a shambles.' Actually, Simon deliberately planned towards that hour in order that his mother should have a highlight in the monotony of the day. It enabled her to arrange her favourite menues with Mrs Jessop, who prided herself on her culinary arts.

'What a lovely idea,' Emma said with enthusiasm.

Verity cried, 'Oh, how like Clare you are ... I always miss her—and Hugh.' She gave a little sigh. 'Have you heard from them?'

'They telephoned from Nairobi the other day. My coming to you delighted them, as you know.' A warm feeling made Emma glow as she thought of her parents. Being separated from them a good deal over the years had, curiously enough, cemented the bond between them; their homecoming was always an event, a celebration, and she, herself, had benefited from their absence, becoming self-reliant and independent as a result.

'You didn't consider joining them?' Simon spoke with a degree of anxiety.

'Only by way of a holiday, should they remain longer than expected.'

'An idea!' he exclaimed with enthusiasm. 'The three of us could go!' He looked at Emma speculatively.

'They are renting a house and would certainly love to have us.' Emma laughed as though she were discussing pie in the sky, her thoughts concerned with Verity. Would she be able to make the journey? A wave of apprehension surged over Emma at the enormity of the task she had undertaken; a task she could not lightly dismiss should any unforeseen problems arise. Mixing family friendships with work might present difficulties, and although circumstances made it *appear* that she knew almost all there was to know about Verity Conway, what would the intimacy of nursing reveal? She noticed how readily Simon had said, '*The three of us*'. Did Verity dominate his life? And suppose he should want to marry? Faint colour crept into her cheeks. Why think of that? She'd only been in the house for about half-an-hour, and already she was analysing and dissecting!

Jessop appeared carrying the tea-tray, placing it on a small table next to Verity's chair. Emma was grateful for the diversion. For a second she gazed around her. The veranda led off the drawing room in which they now sat, and from it the grounds spread out, merging with the undulating countryside. The silence was deep, yet drowsy, broken only by the humming of bees and the song of the birds. Suddenly her gaze was drawn back to Verity who said, 'You're honoured, Emma; Simon hardly ever manages to snatch a cup of tea—at least not here, like this.' She lifted the tea-pot as she spoke, and was about to pour out when, to her dismay, she not only dropped the silver pot, but knew that her aim had been a distance away from her target.

'Oh, *Simon*——' she wailed.

Emma immediately retrieved the pot which was on its side, the tea running through the cups lying in disarray, one broken.

'That's the second time my hand has let me down,' Verity murmured. 'I *loved* pouring out the tea and if

I can't even do *that*——' She stopped, near to tears.

Jessop was summoned and he removed the tray, speedily returning with it newly set.

'Put it by Nurse's chair,' Verity said woodenly.

Emma poured. Simon took the cup and added milk. No sugar. Emma made a note of the fact. But it was as though the skies had darkened, the little blue mists in the valley suddenly had the chill of autumn. Conversation died, and Emma knew that Verity would not take kindly to empty chatter calculated to distract attention from what had occurred. Every now and then she felt her gaze drawn back to Simon, and their eyes looked long and intently at each other, as though that moment was petrified and, from it, magic flowed, drawing them irrevocably together. He got up abruptly, having drunk his tea.

'I'll be back with the others,' he said. 'Have a rest, Mother, before we have those drinks later on; or would you like us to——?'

Verity interrupted almost fiercely, 'Don't dare talk of cancelling the evening. I want Emma to know everyone; she's part of the family now——' She stopped. 'We'll talk about it later,' she added, her voice suddenly flat.

Emma watched and listened, her nursing experience cutting through emotion.

When the tea had been cleared away, Verity asked abruptly, 'Will I lose the use of my hand—my arm?' She hastened, 'And I shall always want the truth from you, Emma—the *truth*——' Her voice had risen, then she paused and said apologetically, almost humbly, 'My dear, I know you can't answer my questions, and that no one can. I've read everything up about M.S. Heaven knows there are enough medical books *here*! The symptoms come and go, and I've tried to learn to live with them, and try not to be a misery. Forgive me if I sometimes fail.'

Emma was touched and she thought how different it was to deal with a patient away from hospital environment. Concentrating on one person could, she realised, be a more exacting task than dealing with many.

'I'm sure you are not likely to be a misery! If you are, I shall consider it my job to shake you out of it.'

'I try to think of Simon.'

The name already had significance and Emma exclaimed, 'He is very concerned for your well-being.'

Verity said suddenly and with a revealing intensity, 'I don't know what I shall do when he marries.'

Emma felt that she was holding her breath, 'Is he likely to be married?'

'If some women had their way—yes.'

'Meaning that doctors are sought after?' Emma spoke lightly.

'In a way, yes. And not always by women most likely to succeed at being a doctor's *wife*.' Verity forced a rather wintry smile.

Was that the possessive mother speaking? Emma could find no answer to the question.

She helped Verity change that evening, Verity's stiff leg, and by no means strong arms, making even the simple tasks connected with dressing both difficult and exhausting.

'Mrs Jessop has been wonderful,' Verity said, 'but

she has more than enough to do. Simon made me see that. Also, that he needs extra help in the practice . . . *I* didn't want you here to help *me*,' she admitted ingenuously.

'Then I must make myself indispensable,' Emma retorted laughingly.

'I feel you are that already,' Verity said with a relieved sigh, as Emma pinned a diamond spray brooch near her neckline and said, 'You look very, very, smart. That goldy colour suits you.'

Verity put out a hand, squeezed Emma's, and murmured, 'Thank you.'

Emma looked around her. It was a very different suite from the one upstairs. Smaller, with more built-in cupboards, and a specially designed dressing table and swivelchair. The sitting room was cream and russet, with chintz covers on sofa and chairs. 'I had those covered specially,' Verity explained, 'so that, should I spill things . . . well, laundry is cheaper than re-upholstering!'

'The garden surrounds you,' Emma said, deliberately changing the subject, 'and everywhere is so light.'

'Too light,' Verity commented ruefully. 'The light hurts my eyes . . . would you pull the blinds down half-way. The evening sun is so *strong* . . . and close the windows on the left. Chilly.' She gave a little shiver. 'And now *you* must go and change.' She smiled as she spoke. 'You have hair just like Clare's—soft, and with the sun on it, streaked with auburn. Can you wear it in any style, too?'

'Yes; which is fortunate in my job!'

'In any job.' Verity added irrelevantly, 'You

wouldn't know you were in a doctor's house, would you? The practice quarters adjoin us. There's a covered walk ... but you'll soon find out for yourself!'

Emma nodded and went upstairs to change. Excitement welled up again as she showered and chose a white dress with embroidered bodice and fitted waist. It had an old-world charm, without looking old-fashioned. How many partners had Simon? Would she like them, and they her? Thus far she had thought only of Verity, now the truth began to dawn that she was about to join a doctor's practice, even if only part-time. The prospect seemed daunting. Yet why? All she was being asked to do was second nature after the years of hospital experience. The thought of Simon lingered. She would be working for *him*, and already he disturbed her, his personality powerful, his manner half-gentle and yet re-inforced with an iron-willed determination. A man, she suspected, who would always get what he wanted.

She stood there in the sun-rifted room, holding her breath for a moment. Her reflection in the floor-to-ceiling looking-glass suggested animation and a breathless expectancy. This, she told herself, was it! The climax of a day which could change her life.

A few minutes later, as she entered the drawing-room, all eyes were turned upon her. Simon detached himself from the little group, and drew her forward.

Emma had an impression of friendliness, the atmosphere welcoming, so that she said, 'This is rather like sitting for one's A levels!'

'Good lord,' a deep voice said, 'not as bad as that. We're really quite a harmless crowd when you get to know us.'

'And *that* is Brett Curzon speaking,' Simon exclaimed. 'He's been with me since we started.'

'It's good to have you here,' Brett Curzon said warmly, giving Emma a rather fierce handshake.

'And I'm Stephen,' a voice put in. 'The surgeon of the outfit . . . not one of the "psychological gentlemen"!'

Simon remained at Emma's elbow and she thought, with relief, that she had now met the partners, and was prepared for the staff. She was already beginning to feel reassured. She studied Brett Curzon. He was shorter than Simon, fair-haired, with friendly blue eyes, and humour lurking at the corners of his generous mouth. Stephen Gilmore was a more sophisticated type, his gaze contemplative and appraising. She had a feeling of relief because it was not a large, impersonal, practice.

At that moment, a tall dark-haired girl came into the room. She had poise and quiet confidence.

'Ah,' Simon said, 'here is the fourth member of the team—Dr Craig—Odile,' he added.

'So sorry I'm late,' Odile said, with a dazzling smile. 'But midders have no respect for time! Mrs Lawson now has a girl, and after three boys it has been something of an occasion!' She looked at Emma and held out her hand, 'I'm sure you're Nurse Reade,' she added with a warm friendliness. 'I'm so glad you are going to help us all.' As she spoke, she half-turned to embrace Verity who was sitting nearby.

'Thank you,' Emma murmured, a little over-whelmed. The thought flashed into her mind: surely Dr Craig didn't come into the category of the women Verity had mentioned in connection with the possibility of Simon marrying?

Almost immediately, Emma was introduced to Mrs Hedley, the practice secretary, a pleasant woman in her late fifties who had built the past few years around Simon, concealing the fact by a governess-like manner and brisk efficiency. Then there was Rose Marlow, her assistant, quick-witted and in her early twenties; and Maude Dexter who made fun of her name, and was a live-wire receptionist-cum-Girl-Friday, appreciated by everyone with whom she came in contact. She was twenty-five, had gone in for nursing, but lacked the discipline necessary to stay the course. Working in her present capacity was a happy compromise. The atmosphere between them all was obviously harmonious, good-natured banter making conversation easy and fluent. Jessop and his wife served the drinks, canapés and delectable items, thought up and executed by Mrs Jessop.

'Well?' Simon asked, moving to Emma's side. 'What do you think of us all?' His smile was infectious.

'Charming, and so friendly.'

'I believe people work better without unnecessary formality.'

'Provided they're efficient.'

'Ah! You remember my mother's remark?'

'Yes . . . this is a splendid way for me to get to know everyone.'

'I'll show you the practice part of the house later on,' he promised. 'And the garden.'

'Thank you.' She looked at him, noting every shade of expression on his face, drawn to him almost against her will as she tried to be natural and relaxed. At that moment she turned slightly, her gaze drawn to Odile Craig who, oblivious of her surroundings, was standing transfixed, looking at Simon with what Emma knew almost with a sense of shock, was love—deep, passionate and fiercely possessive. It was a revelation which projected drama into the situation, although Emma could not have said why. Was Simon involved? There was nothing in his demeanour to suggest that he was even noticing Odile at that second.

The telephone rang and Simon answered it, calling to Odile, 'I'm afraid it's for you!'

Odile seemed to step forward from the shadows, her expression guarded as she took the receiver from Simon's hand. A few seconds later she exclaimed, 'Mrs Mornay has started, and since I promised to deliver her——' She shrugged her shoulders.

'Come back later,' Simon urged.

Odile's laughter was high-pitched, 'Now you're joking! You'll probably all be asleep by the time I'm free.'

'No need to hang around once you've seen her; may be hours,' Simon said confidently.

'You don't know Mrs Mornay,' Odile retorted with a wry smile and, apologising to Verity for leaving so soon, hurried to the door. Simon accompanied her.

Stephen turned to Emma.

'Odile does most of the midder work—very popular and conscientious.'

'And very lovely, too,' Emma said spontaneously.

Stephen looked reflective. 'Yes,' he agreed; 'yes, she is.' He might just have discovered the fact. 'By the way, I had the pleasure of meeting your parents when they came here. You are very like your mother.'

Emma gave a little laugh. 'So everyone tells me; we're often taken for sisters.'

'Do you mind that?'

'Good heavens, no! One is always proud of young parents!' She paused, 'Or do you disagree?'

'On the contrary. But I *have* known of mothers who were jealous of their daughters ... why didn't you become a doctor?'

'Because my ambition was to travel—to see the world in a nurses' uniform!'

Stephen retorted amusedly, 'We're about ninety-four miles from London, so you've made a start!'

They laughed together, and unconsciously looked towards Verity who was in animated conversation with Mrs Hedley.

'I hope,' said Stephen earnestly, 'that very little actual *nursing* will be required.' He sighed. 'Simon has had very little peace of mind recently.'

Emma looked solemn, but made no comment. Sub-consciously she was waiting for Simon to return. The room seemed empty without him. He appeared at that moment, and came to her side. 'With luck Odile may look in later,' he said, his expression eloquent of satisfaction.

Emma felt a slight pang. It was obviously very important to him that Odile should return. Adroitly, she detached herself from both Stephen and Simon, and crossed to Verity's chair, entering into the conversation with Verity and Mrs Hedley, Rose and Maude interjecting the odd remark, obviously enjoying themselves.

'It will be fun having you with us,' Rose exclaimed.

'You make it sound as though there isn't any *work* done in the practice,' Mrs Hedley said admonishingly.

'Now, Mrs Hedley,' Maude piped up, 'we don't want any "governess" talk this evening; do we, Mrs Conway? Everyone knows we work a thirty-six-hour day at Hunter's Close!'

'I know you all work splendidly,' Verity said, swallowing a smile at the 'governess talk'.

Mrs Hedley studied Emma, thinking that she was very young for the work she was about to undertake. The responsibility of an M.S. patient, plus that of checking the practice patients, might well have daunted someone twice her age. Mrs Hedley kept everyone in neat compartments, documented and labelled according to age and proficiency. Rose and Maude always wondered in what category the late lamented Mr Hedley had been docketed, agreeing that Mrs Hedley was a type one could never visualise as a wife; but they respected her, and pandered to her precise little ways, and love of 'neatness'—a word of which she was inordinately fond. By the time the small gathering broke up, Emma felt that she was already part of their team, without fear or strangeness. Brett had the last word with her as he was about to leave, 'Back to the T.P.R's tomorrow, Nurse,' he said in a bantering tone. 'Don't allow us to overwork you.'

'Have you ever met a doctor who *recognised* overwork?' Emma quipped.

'Touché!' he cried.

'You asked for that,' Simon chimed in.

Silence fell for a second or two when the last car
had driven away. The drawing room took to itself
its own personality, the atmosphere peaceful, the
memories pleasant.

'Enjoyable,' Simon said briefly. He looked at
Emma.

'I liked everyone here. I didn't feel a stranger.'

'You,' said Simon, 'could never be a stranger.'

Was it his deep voice that gave the words significance? All Emma knew was that her heart treasured
them, and quickened its beat.

Watching, Verity said, 'I'm tired; I'll have a rest.'
She looked appealingly at Emma who immediately
went to her side. 'My legs get so *stiff*,' Verity
murmured disconsolately, as Emma helped her out
of her chair.

'Even people we like can sometimes be tiring,'
Emma said understandingly.

Simon noticed that his mother made no attempt
to use her stick, but clung to Emma as they went
from the room. And while he was delighted that she
had agreed to accept Emma's help, nevertheless he
did not want her to lose her independent spirit, or
sink into a state of invalidism.

'It seems impossible that you've been with us only
a matter of hours,' he said to Emma later on that
evening, when they were having coffee in the drawing room after dinner.

'The background of family friendships and my coming here for a specific purpose cuts through any strangeness.' She infused a light-hearted note into the remark, finding his steady contemplation of her disconcerting. Simon, she thought, was a man of whom one was continually aware; he made his presence felt through sheer force of personality, irrespective of whether he spoke or not.

'Would you like that Cook's tour?' he asked abruptly.

'Oh, yes. Knowing where one is going actually to work . . . well!' She smiled. 'It will all be very new to me.'

Simon took her into the hall, through a door to the left which led to a glass-covered way that finally adjoined what seemed to her to be another house. There was a reception area; surgery, secretarial quarters, and a common room where, Simon said, 'coffee fiends gather from time to time—myself included!' Attached to it all was a radiology centre. 'That is run by Owen Bradley,' Simon explained. 'Again, it means time saved and diagnosis expedited.' His manner became professional, authoritative. 'And over here we have the consulting rooms . . . this is mine,' he added, opening a door as he spoke. It was a medium sized room, with his desk so placed that the light from the windows (which overlooked an orchard) fell on the patient. Shades of cream and russet again predominated, merging unobtrusively with the medical necessities which constituted furniture.

'That,' said Emma, pointing to what was obviously the patients' chair, 'being the confessional!'

Simon flashed her an amused glance. 'One way of putting it.' He opened a door into the examining room. 'You will sometimes use this to take blood pressure, etcetera, before I see the patient. And you'll keep the charts. Until you've familiarised yourself with the routine, I'm detailing you to attend to my patients only.' His manner at that moment seemed almost stern, and Emma felt suddenly, unexpectedly, trapped. Had she been mad to come to Hunter's Close? Family ties and hospitality tied her, no matter what the job might entail. And already this man excited her; his strength challenging and, curiously enough, awakening a mood of aggression because of her own vulnerability.

'Surgery,' he went on, 'will not clash with my mother's requirements. She always has her breakfast in bed, and seldom gets up before ten-thirty. Evening surgery is at a time when she is resting before dinner. Beyond that, we shall have to adjust things as we go.'

Emma's chaotic emotions reduced her to silence.

'Well?' The query hinted that he expected some comment.

Emma said hastily, 'I understand. Everything here is suggestive of great precision—I come back to your mother's word, "efficiency".'

'You cannot have a well-run practice without it,' he said firmly. 'And it's my contention that patients have a right to expect it.'

'Are your partners married?' The question rushed out.

'Brett is; he and Gail, his wife, have two daughters. Stephen's a bachelor.'

Emma asked breathlessly, 'And Dr Craig?'

'Odile?' He repeated the name with a certain significance.

'Is *she* married?'

Surprise betrayed itself in his vigorous, 'Good lord, no . . . shall we have a look at the garden? The light is going.'

They wandered out across the smooth lawns. The sweet, damp earth held the fragrance of a day that had been sun-drenched. Trees shivered faintly in the breeze like a lullaby, and everywhere around them roses were massed. Flowering shrubs formed cascades, while macrocarpyre hedges led to informal gardens, one containing a lily pond. Unexpected little paths took them finally into the cool twilight of a nearby woodland. The sky was fired by a sunset that sprayed the wispy clouds with crimson, softest rose and, here and there, bays of blue completed the giant mural on which a crescent moon was etched in gold. There was an unearthly radiance about it all— romantic and enchanting—as the tall trees towered above them. And all the time Emma was conscious of the man walking beside her; his strong features outlined in the dusk; and as she studied him, he turned and met her gaze. Just then she stumbled and he caught her arm, his touch electric, as she saw the unmistakable passion in his eyes. Silence held them; the magic of approaching night bringing its own temptation. For a breathless moment she thought he was going to kiss her, but he drew back, releasing her as he said tensely, 'We must go in. My mother may need you.'

Emma's cheeks flamed. This was a new and shat-

tering experience. There'd been mild harmless flir-
tations during her hospital years, but never an ex-
plosive emotion such as this, leaving her trembling,
her heart beating wildly.

Very little was said on the way back to the house.
Emma went immediately to Verity's room. She felt
self-conscious, almost as though her thoughts were
tangible and Verity could read them.

Verity said brightly, 'And what do you think of
Hunter's Close now that you've seen it all?'

'It's beautiful; and the practice quarters must be
quite unique. There's nothing cold or clinical about
them, and yet one knows they are perfectly
managed.'

'Simon was the architect of it all. He has a way
with the practice—and with people.' Verity said
slowly, 'Did you see Odile's cottage?'

'No,' Emma said, startled.

'You can see its upper windows from your bedroom—through the trees. It's just where the wood
begins, but you wouldn't notice it unless it was
pointed out to you.'

Emma wondered why, even in that short while,
Odile's name brought a feeling of unease.

'Very handy for her,' Emma said, trying to keep
her voice steady.

'It was a gardener's cottage which Simon converted and enlarged. Very attractive and, as you say,
"handy".'

Why hadn't Simon mentioned it? Emma asked
herself, and knew that there was no reason why he
should have done so. She left Verity's room a little
later and went very slowly upstairs.

Simon stood watching her from the landing. When she reached his side their eyes met.

'Goodnight, Emma,' he said softly. 'I'm so glad you're here.'

'So am I,' she whispered.

She went almost blindly into her room, moving instinctively to the window. Lights twinkled from Odile's cottage and as she watched, seemingly rooted to the spot, she saw Simon's tall figure striding towards it.

In that moment she asked herself how it would be possible to live in the same house with such a man, and not fall in love with him. . . .

CHAPTER TWO

EMMA adapted herself to life at Hunter's Close with apparent ease, finding her tasks exacting, but interesting. Simon's presence high-lighted each day, giving the hours emotional significance, despite her endeavour to regard him dispassionately. He was, she argued, simply her employer, their friendship fortuitous. Nevertheless her pulse quickened at his footstep, and at the sound of his voice and, even now, as she presided over the tea-tray and attended to Verity, she was anticipating his presence.

'You've put *sugar* in my tea,' Verity exclaimed with distaste, flashing Emma a critical look. 'You *know* how I hate it, Emma!'

Simon overheard the remark as he entered the

drawing room from the terrace.

'Our nurse is very absent-minded today,' he said in a tone that dragged Emma's spirits down to disaster level. It didn't help to know it was true, and that her concentration had been upon him at the expense of efficiency.

'I'm sorry,' she murmured, cheeks flushed, and feeling like a gauche schoolgirl. She poured out another cup of tea and took it to Verity.

Coolly, imperturbably, Simon rang the bell, and when Jessop appeared, ordered another cup which, when brought, he filled himself and settled in his particular chair. He looked across at Emma, his gaze penetrating.

Verity noticed, without comment, that since Emma's advent, Simon had taken to joining them for tea whenever possible, instead of having a cup taken to his consulting room by a solicitous Mrs Hedley. Verity was astonished by his overt criticism of Emma and hastened, 'In this heat we may all be forgiven for our shortcomings. I snapped just now.' She smiled at Emma, her manner apologetic.

Simon made no comment, but finished his tea, set the cup somewhat deliberately on the tray, and as he stepped on to the terrace, said, 'I'd like a word with you before surgery, Emma.' His voice was neither condemnatory, nor conciliatory, but there was a stillness about him that seemed ominous.

'I never know quite what to make of my son in this mood,' Verity said unexpectedly. The 'my son' sounded significant.

What, Emma asked herself frantically, had she done, or left undone, to merit his accusation of absent-mindedness? It seemed that in the space of a few minutes, he had vanished from her world. Ridiculous, she argued, detesting any suggestion of spinelessness. She lifted her chin a few inches higher when, some ten minutes later, she entered Simon's consulting room. If he thought he could intimidate her, he was wrong! She was always ready to acknowledge her mistakes and to apologise . . . She was acutely aware of him as he sat at his desk. His lightweight suit—a soft grey with matching shirt—became him, emphasising his good looks. It was impossible to gauge his feelings as he said, 'Sit down, Emma.' He indicated the patients' chair, studying her with a perceptive gaze.

'Is anything worrying you?' he asked unexpectedly, his voice quiet, yet firm.

It was the last question she had anticipated and her defiant aggression slid away.

' "Worrying me"?' she echoed. 'No! Oh, no!'

'And no one has upset you?' He might have been the doctor humouring a patient.

'No.' She hastened, 'Everyone has been wonderful—helpful in every way.'

A flicker of surprise went over his face.

'Then having established that, can you tell me why you have been so preoccupied and forgetful these past two days? I hope I'm human enough to allow for any reasonable lapse, but I cannot overlook inefficiency.' His manner was direct and commanding.

It was as though Emma suddenly came out of a trance as she put a hand up to her cheek in a moment of appalled recollection.

'Mrs *Watkins*,' she gasped. 'I *forgot* her.'

'Yes, Emma; you forgot her. And why put her in the emergency waiting room?'

Emma looked dazed. Why indeed, she asked herself, and could find no answer.

'She'd been there nearly an hour when Odile found her—and then only because Odile, herself, wanted her patient to wait while an appointment was made with Owen. By that time you were out with my mother. If Mrs Watkins hadn't been the long-suffering type, she would have raised the roof— and rightly so.'

Emma made a helpless gesture. 'I'm so *sorry*.' Her heart was pounding, embarrassment and apology merged into total confusion.

'So am I,' he said, his words seeming like a whip-lash. He shook his head and surveyed her critically. 'I'd come to rely on you . . .. And Mrs Watkins isn't all. You didn't put out Mr Portman's notes, or use your initiative over Miss Demby. She is the popper-in-for-a-chat-patient. I told you to do a routine check and that I'd see her next time.'

'That,' Emma said swiftly, 'I misunderstood . . . the rest I've no excuses for——' Her voice shook slightly.

'Then I'm glad to be spared them. And you cannot afford to *misunderstand* instructions.' His tone was solemn, and at the same time puzzled, his brows puckered. 'What concerns me is *why*—why this sudden unaccountable lapse after such an auspicious beginning? Everything has gone so smoothly——' He got up from his desk as he spoke and moved towards the window, looking back at her. 'There must be *something*——'

His tall figure stood there—a challenge—awakening emotion so fierce that her body trembled and she dare not meet his eyes in case he saw the message written in her own. She didn't pretend to understand the power he exerted over her, or why, suddenly, inexplicably, it had robbed her of normal concentration, swirling her into a fantasy world where only he existed. Now, his anger and bewilderment stabbed her, the more so since the obvious initial attraction between them had been overwhelming, giving significance to every look, and ecstasy to every inadvertent touch.

He almost turned on her as he said fiercely, 'I don't want this to be a failure . . . can't you *see*? And if there's a reason rather than an excuse, tell me.'

As he spoke their eyes met, their gaze deep and entreating. For a second she hardly dared to breathe as passion held them, their physical awareness of each other as acute as pain. Then, drawing on all her courage and resolution, she managed to say, 'It isn't always possible to give reasons, Simon.'

He startled her by demanding, 'Has it anything to do with Stephen? I certainly didn't judge you to be unreliable, but if——'

She cut in, amazed, 'Stephen?'

'Why not? You've become very friendly . . . had dinner with him.' At that point Simon stopped, realising that he was putting himself at a disadvantage and taking authority too far. 'I'm sorry,' he murmured almost stiffly, 'I'm presuming on friendship.'

Emma made a little gesture of denial.

'I promise I shall not fall down on my job again.'

He looked at her with unnerving intensity, 'Please don't, Emma . . .'

'I won't.' Her voice was soft. Then, 'Whatever must Odile have thought of me?'

'Odile?' he echoed, amused. 'What about poor Mrs Watkins?'

'Was she very angry?'

'Amazingly, no! She thought you looked as though you "had something on your mind". Understanding woman, Mrs Watkins.'

Emma flushed, murmured something about making sure that Verity was all right, reached the door, paused and said, 'Thank you, Simon.'

'I'm doing surgery this evening . . . get back and give me a hand. Oh, and see if Owen's got those X-rays of Mrs Arlett. I'm not very happy about her.' He gave a sigh which indicated concern and with which Emma was now familiar.

Relief surged between them because harmony had been restored. The smile that touched his lips held the intimacy of a caress.

Verity said, 'What did Simon want?' There was just the faintest note of authority in her voice.

'To point out things I'd neglected,' Emma replied.

Verity looked knowing. 'I warned you of his insistence on efficiency.' She gave a little laugh, 'Don't let him brow-beat you.'

'I deserved his criticism.'

'I cannot believe that,' Verity said with emphasis.

'Not even after my having put sugar in your tea!'

'Oh, that——' Verity dismissed it and then

suddenly frowned as she exclaimed, 'My arm feels stiff today, and I didn't notice it at all yesterday. Why don't they know anything about this disease? I get so impatient about it all.' She paused and then said with disconcerting directness, 'Do you think Simon is impatient with me?'

Emma didn't hesitate, 'That's the last thing ... his only concern is your well-being.'

'I appreciate his thoughtfulness, but I often wish I could know what he really *thinks* ... does he—does he talk to you about me?' The question had an adolescent implication and a sub-conscious desire for flattery.

Emma replied guardedly, 'Only insofar as your comfort——'

Verity made a little deprecating gesture, '*Comfort*, *health* ... I feel like an exhibit.' Her voice rose slightly. 'Solicitude can stifle one like a blanket. I don't want to lose my *identity*. And don't you humour me as though I were an imbecile child!' The words were shrill and, for a second, startling.

Emma's voice was matter-of-fact, cool, 'All I'm going to do is to see you to your room, and then help Simon with surgery. It's far too hot for tantrums this evening.' With that she stooped and levered Verity to a standing position, aware of Verity's defensive, defiant expression, but not alarmed by it, even though it was the first evidence of such a swiftly changing mood.

'I don't see why Simon needs you to help him with surgery.' It was a blunt aggressive statement, which Emma ignored. '*I* need you. I'm hot and I'd like a shower.'

'I'll give you one as usual, later on before dinner.'

Verity's look was piercing, 'It is not for you to tell *me*,' she snapped, but nevertheless went quietly to her suite, allowing Emma to settle her on the bed.

So, Emma reflected, the pattern was beginning to emerge. How far was this temperamental see-saw a matter of genetic influence, character? And how much the result of personality changes due to the disease? Even rationalising the incident did not automatically remove its sting.

It was a heavy surgery. Simon was a great favourite, and Emma realised that certain patients manoeuvred so that they came when he was 'on', consequently the waiting room bulged, patients cosily nattering about their respective ailments, and eulogising 'Dr Conway' as though he were a heart-throb film star.

'Miss Thornby—the last,' Emma said, finally.

Simon frowned.

'Miss Thornby,' he echoed almost belligerently, then added forcefully, 'I'd like you to stay around here while I deal with her.'

Emma arched her eyebrows.

'The practice menace?' she suggested.

'In every way,' he said meaningfully.

'Don't worry,' Emma laughed, 'I'll be there if you need to scream for help! I've dealt with a few nymphomaniacs in hospital. The doctors used to be scared to death!'

'And well they might be . . . bring her in.'

Violet Thornby cherished the illusion that she was highly attractive to men, and her endless psychosomatic ailments ensured that 'the doctor' took due notice of her. She was emotionally immature, and had a highly inflamed imagination where all sexual matters were concerned. She was convinced that Simon nurtured a secret passion for her which he was far too honourable to betray, but that a little encouragement and persuasion might overcome his scruples. The sight of Emma at the instrument trolley dismayed her.

Simon was brisk, professional. What was wrong?

'A pain in my side, Dr Conway.'

Always, Simon thought, something that required an examination! But he was cautious with patients of the Thornby type, because it was perilously easy to overlook a genuine symptom.

'Nurse will attend to you——' He indicated the examining room. 'Then we'll see what's wrong.'

'But——' Her expression of disappointment was obvious.

Simon appeared to be intent upon some notes.

Emma made sure that Miss Thornby revealed only the minimum of flesh necessary for the examination, drawing up the blanket which Miss Thornby would have discarded.

There was no evidence of any trouble, and Simon's manner was precise and wooden. The fluttering eyelashes and cooing voice made no impression.

'I wanted to *talk* to you, Dr Conway.'

Simon pulled the blanket up to Miss Thornby's chin in a gesture of finality.

'No evidence whatever of any inflammation; no tenderness; no distension. You could put on a little weight——'

'Put *on*! But Dr Conway, you surely don't suggest that I should get *fat*.'

'No,' Simon retorted; 'neither do I suggest that you remain thin . . .' He nodded to Emma as if to say, 'that's over!', and walked back to his consulting room.

The platinum blonde head on the examining couch tossed itself in a gesture of annoyance. Frustration was written all over the carefully made-up face. She glared at Emma.

Dressed, and back in the patients' chair, Miss Thornby demanded, 'Are you going to give me something for the pain?'

'No, Miss Thornby; I've satisfied myself that all is well——'

'Why is that nurse here? I—I don't like her being here . . . surely she can——'

'Nurse Reade is working for me permanently,' Simon said with a smile.

'You mean she will always be here when I come?'

'Yes.' Simon got to his feet as he spoke.

'But Dr Conway, I've *known* you . . . I mean, we are *friends*,' she cooed significantly, 'and——' She looked at him appealingly.

'I'm afraid I have a sick patient to visit, Miss Thornby . . .. Now, if you'll excuse me.' He walked to the door and opened it, giving her a polite smile as he did so.

Tears, which Miss Thornby could conjure up on all and sundry occasions, brimmed into her accusing eyes.

'If *you* won't look after me properly, I shall have

to find another doctor,' she protested, chin quivering.

Simon longed to say, 'Can I count on that?', but instead he replied, 'That is your privilege.'

For an agonising second he thought she was going to throw her arms around his neck as she hesitated in the doorway, but she went out, handkerchief fluttering.

'Now,' Emma said, 'I get your point.'

'Pain in her *side*,' Simon muttered under his breath. 'She's a pain in the *neck*!'

'Will she find another doctor?'

'Regretfully, no! She's tried more doctors than a leopard has spots.'

Emma flashed him a smile. 'The attraction of your profession.'

'God knows why!' He added wryly, 'At least we're not heroes to nurses!'

The atmosphere between them until that moment had been natural, professional. They worked together in complete harmony—Emma having accustomed herself to his method, and the manner in which he dealt with his patients. But suddenly, the note of intimacy crept back, and personalities emerged.

'That's generalisation,' Emma said quietly. 'Not altogether valid. Nurses have been known to marry doctors.'

The words came spontaneously, unguardedly, and she turned away from him almost immediately, busying herself with the few remaining tasks of the evening.

His voice came to her on a low, attractive note,

'Then, as a doctor, I must take heart from the fact
... thank you for your moral support. I must go to
see that genuinely sick patient—Mr Brandon, the
emphysema case.'

'Stephen's patient—in hospital.'

'Yes ... I've known him for some years. It cheers
him to realise that I haven't forgotten.'

Emma reflected that the gesture summed up
Simon's character, both as a man and a doctor. She
dragged her thoughts away from him, almost as
though he were a drug on which she had become
dependent. Her own question, asked that first night
at Hunter's Close, re-echoed: 'How would it be possible to live in the same house with such a man, and
not fall in love with him?'

Simon's voice broke into her reverie, 'Hadn't you
better attend to my mother now?'

Emma started guiltily. She had forgotten Verity!

Simon stared after her as she hurried away. The
faraway expression in her eyes—now all too familiar
to him—awakened suspicions he could not avoid, or
overcome. It gave her an elusive quality, all the more
intriguing—and, he had to admit, annoying.

Verity sustained her truculent mood throughout the
rest of the evening. Even the silences seemed to be
filled with a sound like that of a cracked record.
Simon tried to draw her out, inquiring about the
afternoon run and receiving almost the complaint
that they'd gone through Broadway.

'Did you *have* to?' Simon asked. 'Broadway is to
be visited early in the morning, before the tourists
arrive; or on a winter's day.'

Verity protested, 'I used very nearly to *climb* that six hundred feet from the Lygon Arms to the Little Fish Inn—the views over to the Malvern Hills were wonderful . . .. Now what can I do? Sit in the car and look? No thank you. I don't know why we *went* there. Why did we, Emma?'

Emma didn't reply, 'Because you said you wanted to go,' and in the second that she tried to think of a discreet answer, Verity added crossly, 'Or have you forgotten that, too?'

Simon made an exclamation of rebuke; he was shocked, and glanced at Emma half-inquiringly, half-critically. But he tried, nevertheless, to redeem the situation by saying, 'You will probably be able to walk perfectly well in a few weeks . . .'

'Don't be so ridiculous!' Verity glared at him. '*I* shan't have any remissions. Remissions—that's the sop you doctors give M.S. cases . . . and I'd like to talk to you, Simon—alone.' She looked at Emma. 'I'll let you know when I'm ready for bed.'

Emma got up immediately, inclined her head, and went from the room.

'What is all this?' Simon demanded. 'Why speak to Emma in that fashion?'

'Because she's made me angry today; very angry. Forgotten all about *my* needs . . . I wanted a shower before she helped you with surgery . . . wouldn't help me; told me to *wait* . . . oh, yes she did.'

Simon had never seen Verity in this mood, and a weight seemed to crush his heart. It was one thing to have a pleasant invalid, but quite a different matter to have a difficult one.

'You usually have a shower before you change in

the evening,' he reminded her.

'Don't make excuses for her. She told me that you'd been annoyed with her. I'm not a fool.'

'Then don't behave foolishly,' Simon admonished. 'Grievances should be aired and then forgotten. I thought you were so happy and thankful to have Emma here. If I'm wrong, then we'd better do something about it.'

Verity's eyes filled with tears and she hung her head in a pathetic, helpless gesture.

'I'd be lost without her now,' she murmured, raising her gaze to his and then adding urgently, 'Simon?'

'Yes?' He tensed, and waited apprehensively for the question.

'Shall I change? Become difficult? Does it affect people mentally?'

Simon had avoided dwelling on the emotional instability, and pathological optimism, that was often present in multiple sclerosis. He endeavoured to be as honest as possible, knowing Verity might see through subterfuge.

'Some patients tend to dramatise events, become emotional; but temperament plays a big part.'

'Then I must guard against——' She paused, and went on jerkily, 'I haven't been too much of a nuisance so far, have I?' There was a pleading note in her voice.

Simon answered her emphatically. '"Nuisance" doesn't come into it . . .. And now, how about our going out to dinner one night this week?'

'And take Emma,' she said immediately.

'By all means,' he agreed. At that moment he

noticed Emma walking slowly across the lawn, her figure blurred in the gathering dusk.

Verity followed his gaze. 'Would you ask her to forgive me, and say that I'd like to go to bed now?'

As Verity watched Simon move away, the terrifying thought stabbed: was she subconsciously jealous of Emma? The very possibility appalled her, and she thrust it from her mind.

Emma was thinking of Odile as Simon came towards her; re-living the events of that first evening when she had realised Odile's love for Simon. There had been no evidence, so far, that Simon was emotionally involved with Odile and she, Emma, had merely touched the surface of a relationship with Odile.

'You look very pensive,' Simon observed as he reached Emma's side.

'Actually, I was thinking of Odile.'

'Why Odile?' He sounded surprised.

'I don't *know* her any better than when I came here.' Emma hastened, 'That isn't a complaint, or criticism.'

'Odile doesn't make friends easily . . . you would know if she disliked you!'

'Oh, I wasn't thinking of that. She is always very pleasant when I *do* see her, which isn't often.' What, Emma asked herself, were Simon's feelings towards Odile? Colour crept into her cheeks as she dwelt on the possibilities. How often did he visit the cottage? And what had it to do with her? Yet the thought of him with another woman seemed to press a weight on her heart. His nearness was a sweet torture. The twilight was a mosaic of gold and dark purple, as the afterglow spread its radiance.

'Dusk is a beautiful illusion,' Simon murmured with sudden emotion.

'So is life, sometimes.'

'In moments like these, reality is an impostor.' His voice, deep, intense, sent a little shiver over her.

The grounds stretched mysteriously, the approaching night warm and sensuous. Passion held them, suspense unbearable. Simon could not bring himself to mention Verity, or break the spell.

But Emma cried, as he put out his hand to touch hers, 'I must go in——'

'No! *Emma*——' his voice was hoarse.

She almost ran away, lost in the shadows.

Seeing Emma as she stepped into the drawing room, held up the mirror to Verity, reminding her of her own lost youth, and the breathless wonder of being in love. If Simon could put stars in Emma's eyes, what of tomorrow? Verity could hardly bear the spectre of loneliness, or endure the threat to her security. Simon represented that security, which now seemed at risk.

'Such a heavenly night,' Emma exclaimed, trying to keep her voice from shaking. 'Do you feel like going out? It's warm, and——'

'No, thank you,' Verity interrupted. 'Bed and television—there's a good play on.'

Simon sauntered in, his gaze seeking Emma's in a moment of heavy silence.

Emma, heart thudding, helped Verity to her feet.

Verity said to Simon as she and Emma moved to the door, 'Come in a little later to make sure my television is right.'

'I will.' It was a nightly ritual. The television had an automatic control and seldom varied.

After Verity was settled, Simon met Emma in the hall, their awareness of each other immediate.

'I've been thinking,' he began, his manner controlled, 'are we expecting too much of you?'

'In what way?' Her expression held apprehension.

'That you have a great deal to cope with. Verity—helping me in the practice. Long hours—when it really comes to it.'

She flashed, freezing at the possibility of not being satisfactory, 'Just because I had one lapse ... I thought it was all settled and——'

He cut in, emotion whipping up anger, 'That has nothing to do with it .... May I not be *concerned* for you?'

'I'm sorry,' she apologised.

'It is easy to take things for granted when everything goes smoothly,' he insisted.

'After hospital life, being here is a holiday,' Emma assured him. 'Verity merely needs helping; and driving the car—well! I love driving, anyway.' She hesitated, and then added with conviction, 'Working for you is so interesting, too. I'm involved with the patients and have learned a great deal.'

'I'm glad you feel that way ... it consoles me.'

Would he suggest a last drink? Even a walk in what, now, was bright moonlight? She waited on the edge of hope.

But Simon said lightly, 'I'm going over to the cottage. Odile had an emergency and I want a report on it.'

'Goodnight,' Emma exclaimed precipitately, as she began to walk towards the stairs. Her voice was unconsciously frosty.

'Rather early for bed, surely? It's only half-past nine.'

'I like to read.' It was a no-nonsense statement of fact. She began to mount the stairs, aware that he was standing watching her. She did not look back when she reached the landing. The thought, swirling uneasily, was: why couldn't he telephone Odile? What had previously been ecstasy, became half-annoyance and disappointment. Once in her room, she resolutely resisted the impulse to go to the window to watch Simon leave the house. It was no business of hers what he did . . .. She drew in her breath sharply, and then sighed. Would he have kissed her, had she remained just a few more seconds when his hand almost touched hers, as they stood together in the enchanted twilight? Her body heated at the possibility, and she hated the idea that she had run away like a scared adolescent. *Simon!* The name filled her horizon, his presence hypnotic. A little later she got into bed, determined to read, but the words became jumbled in emotional turmoil. Impatiently, she made her way to the window and sat there, hidden by the curtains—now drawn back—as she waited for his return. After what seemed an eternity his tall figure emerged from the shadows. There was the grace of an athlete in his movements as he walked purposefully, appearing lost in thought, and only when he reached the house did he hesitate, and glance up at her window. There was no light on in her room—other than that from the moon—and she pressed further back against the curtains. Then, slowly, dreamily, she returned to bed and slept.

Stephen caught up with her the following morning after surgery as they went into the common room.

'I swear you have the power to disappear at will,' he challenged.

'On my broomstick,' she tossed at him.

'I haven't set eyes on you since last Christmas,' he insisted absurdly.

They laughed together.

'And, with luck,' she suggested, 'you may not do so again until next Christmas!'

'Dinner,' he said emphatically. 'How about going to Stratford—dinner, and the theatre?'

'I'm a working girl—remember?'

'All working girls have time off,' he flashed back. Odile heard the remark as she joined them.

'I second that.' She smiled at Emma. 'I've hardly *seen* you since your arrival—how long ago?'

'Ten weeks,' Emma said. 'It doesn't seem possible that we are nearing the end of August.'

'And talking of dinner,' Odile went on, 'how about coming to me one evening? See the cottage. Ridiculous your not having been there.'

Emma asked herself: Had Simon stimulated the invitation? 'I'd love to come,' she said, and meant it, even if there was a degree of curiosity in the acceptance.

'At least *your* invitation is received with alacrity,' Stephen pointed out. 'Obviously "working girls" can get off for your benefit.' He looked at Odile, a faint smile on his face.

Brett rushed in at that moment. 'Coffee?' he demanded.

Maude appeared as though summoned by radar.

'Coffee,' she said with a grin, 'only don't imagine you have time to drink it. Mrs Seymour has just arrived.'

'She wouldn't grudge me two minutes,' Brett retorted.

'Mrs Seymour would grudge you one bird seed!'

'A good thing it is not part of my diet, then!' Brett sipped the coffee which was hot, made a face and asked, 'Where's the ice? Phew! Can't you make this stuff with *warm* water?'

'Dr Conway insists on his coffee being *hot*.'

Stephen laughed. 'That way, it keeps better while it's getting cold!' His smile suddenly vanished. 'I lost Mrs Herrick this morning,' he said quietly.

They all looked at him. Death was not an easily accepted thing, but a personal blow. Mrs Herrick was one of the 'specials'—a brave woman who had died of carcinoma of the abdomen. Stephen had performed a laparotomy, but the growth was too diffuse to remove.

Emma thought, as she stood there, that doctors might be forgiven their moments of levity.

Brett managed to gulp his coffee. 'Don't forget we're having a confab with Simon at midday,' he said significantly, glancing from Stephen to Odile and, lastly, at Emma. 'Has he alerted you?'

Emma stiffened, feeling a degree of alarm.

'Why, no.'

'He will.' With that Brett strode out.

'Is anything wrong?' Emma asked fearfully.

Odile flashed a meaningful smile at Stephen, 'Just management problems, and an idea I am going to put forward . . .. How is Verity this morning?'

'Having trouble with her right hand again; otherwise well.'

Odile made a sympathetic, but unintelligible, utterance, finishing with, 'And we're absolutely useless when it comes really to helping her. It infuriates me.' With that she went from the room.

'A dedicated doctor,' Stephen said admiringly. 'And a fighter.'

'I should imagine so,' Emma agreed, feeling suddenly flat.

Odile returned unexpectedly—just standing in the doorway. 'How about Wednesday evening?' she suggested, addressing Emma. 'If we don't fix a date, we shall never get together.'

'Subject to it being satisfactory to Verity,' Emma agreed. 'Thank you.'

'I'll deal with Verity,' Odile said with a confident smile.

And again, Emma wondered if Simon had inspired the invitation.

Just before midday, when Simon returned from his visits, he hurried into the drawing room where Verity and Emma were sitting, and said urgently, 'There's a gathering of the clans in my consulting room and I'd like you to be there, Emma. You are part of the practice and it's good for you to know what's going on . . .. You'll be all right, Mother?'

'Perfectly.' Inwardly, Verity wondered if Simon

was wise to include Emma in the partners' day-to-day problems. In addition, she didn't want Emma to be allocated extra work which would rob her, Verity, of Emma's help and attention. Emma had become a companion as well as her nurse, and Verity was jealous of the advantage.

Simon's manner was purely professional as he and Emma walked from the house to the practice quarters. He mentioned an appointment he wanted her to make, and a new patient due that afternoon.

'Mrs Leighton,' Emma said. 'I spoke to her.'

'Of course you did . . .' He opened his consulting-room door, and stood back for Emma to precede him. There was not a flicker of emotion in the look he gave her.

Brett, Stephen and Odile were already waiting.

'Sorry to be late,' Simon said.

Odile laughed. 'No alibi needed; we belong to the "always late club".'

They discussed various aspects of the practice, agreed on a few changes, and then Odile became spokesman as she said, 'And now I'd like to talk about Emma.' She flashed Emma a friendly glance as she spoke.

'Emma?' Simon was instantly alert, almost challenging.

'She has been here about ten weeks,' Odile pointed out, 'and we're wondering if, now that she has obviously grasped the ramifications of the job, she might not work with, and for, us all, Simon, instead of solely for you.' Odile added swiftly, 'I know your idea was to ease her in, but——' she paused discreetly before continuing, 'but I'm sure you haven't overlooked the fact that it *was* originally intended that Emma should generally assist in the practice. I should be thankful for a little help, particularly as my work is almost entirely among women patients, and my list has grown, as you know.'

Simon stood there, shocked. He *had* conveniently forgotten that Emma was intended as a *practice* acquisition, and not for his sole benefit. The 'easing her in' had been an agreed policy. Instead, he had monopolised her services.

Emma's heart sank and she hung on Simon's reply, clinging to the fact that he was the senior partner, and if he wanted her to devote her time to him, he could say so! Emotion, fear, hope, built up in desperation.

But Simon didn't hesitate.

'You're right, of course. I'm afraid I've lost track of time.'

Odile was relieved, and therefore expansive, 'It has struck me that the room next to mine might make an ideal place in which Emma could work, and see the patients before they reach us. One or two things need doing, otherwise it couldn't be better ...' She looked at Simon first, then at the others, and back to Simon. 'What do you think?'

Emma heard Simon's brisk words, 'An excellent idea', rather like a death knell.

CHAPTER THREE

STEPHEN broke the heavy silence that followed Simon's approval and said, 'How do you feel about it, Emma?'

Emma drew on courage and a determination not to betray her disappointment.

'I agree with Simon. It's an excellent idea. After all, I came here to work in the *practice*.'

'But not,' Simon said forcefully, 'to be *over*worked. A rota system will have to be thought up. I appreciate all you said, Odile. You've taken the brunt of many things recently, and now that we're sliding down into autumn, we must get everything sorted out for the maximum efficiency. I'll fit in with whatever you decide and arrange.' He looked at Emma and smiled. 'And I'm sure you will do the same.'

'With pleasure,' she replied, feeling low, dispirited. Simon seemed to be a stranger. Yet why had he kept her with him so long? And why had Odile taken it upon herself to point the situation out to him? A room next to Odile—not to Simon. It seemed like being banished to the North Pole, and a sick sensation settled in the pit of her stomach. Her mouth felt dry. If only Simon had been defensive, shown some regret at the idea of their relationship changing. She ridiculed herself for her stupidity. She had merely spared him *work*; made life that much easier. On reflection, it was the best thing that could happen.

It would prevent her concentration upon him, empty her head and her heart of their foolish romantic notions. It wasn't as if she disliked Odile, either. Nevertheless, Odile would, of necessity, find some satisfaction in breaking up the exclusive Doctor–Nurse relationship. Every shade of expression on Odile's face, as she looked at Simon, betrayed an intensity of emotion which, Emma argued, only she, as a woman, would recognise.

Simon uttered the last chilling words, 'Then we've had a very successful meeting.' His laugh came spontaneously, 'Not that I can recall any unsuccessful ones.'

Brett nodded. 'But God help us if the women team up on us!'

Odile drew Emma aside while the men went into a huddle. 'We can talk things over when you come to the cottage on Wednesday. I'm so glad Simon agreed about the room. It will give you independence, and somewhere to spread yourself . . . or will you miss working almost exclusively for him?'

Emma felt that Odile was waiting anxiously for the answer, and said easily, 'Nurses are used to working with, and for, everyone . . . I'm sure Brett and Stephen will be easy to get on with.'

'Oh, they're wonderful. In fact, less exacting than Simon.' A smile touched Odile's lips as she added, 'And I'm not difficult—the girls will vouch for me!'

'True,' Emma agreed. 'They already have. Mrs Hedley, Rose, and Maude are genuine fans of yours.'

'Then I must preen myself—makes me feel like a film star! But we all love a little praise . . . now I must fly.' She moved swiftly to Simon's side, glanced at Brett and Stephen, before saying to Simon, 'I'll see you at Mrs Mornay's——' she touched his shoulder as she spoke. It was a fleeting gesture which Emma did not miss.

Brett and Stephen had appointments, also, and moved to the door. Stephen shot a significant look at Emma, 'Don't forget Stratford and the theatre.'

'I won't,' Emma promised, a little defiantly.

Simon and Emma were left alone in what, to her, seemed an empty world.

'Well, Emma?' Simon was watchful.

'I'm going to dinner and the theatre with Stephen, when it can be arranged.'

'So I gathered . . . you will like a room to yourself in the practice,' he added.

He spoke *for* her, taking her reaction for granted, and a flicker of resentment crossed her features, but she said, 'It was a good idea of Odile's.'

They stood there like two strangers looking at each other across a chasm.

'Now, I must be joining Odile at Mrs Mornay's— we're worried about her.'

'Wasn't that the patient Odile delivered the first evening I came to Hunter's Close?' Emma exclaimed.

'You've an excellent memory. Yes. She's pregnant again and not, at the moment, fit to cope with the early symptoms. In fact, she thought her family was complete—she now has two boys and two girls; even so, she doesn't want to miscarry.'

At that moment Emma was not interested in Mrs Mornay. Her thoughts centred around the recently-made arrangements.

'Shall I be working entirely for the others and not for you at all?' she asked abruptly.

Simon's expression was impassive.

'It will depend on the work load. But I'd like you to give Odile as much help as you can.'

'Give her priority, in fact?'

'You could put it that way . . . I must be off.'

'You've four appointment patients this afternoon, the first at two o'clock,' she reminded him. 'That includes Mrs Leighton, the new patient we've already mentioned.'

'And you're taking Mother into Cheltenham,' he said, and studied Emma speculatively, adding with sudden enthusiasm, 'I'll try to join you both when you get back. Snatch a cup of tea.'

The words cut through her depression. She walked beside him to the door which he opened for her, and looking down at her with a deep reflective gaze, he said tensely, 'I shall miss you.'

They were the last words she had expected him to utter, and the ones she most longed to hear.

She didn't speak, but glanced up at him before hurrying away.

Simon appeared at tea time, and the words, '*I shall miss you*', seemed to echo between them as his gaze met hers.

'Emma tells me she is to have her own room, and stop being your nurse exclusively,' Verity said with some deliberation. 'Will that work?'

Simon was immediately alert. 'Why shouldn't it?' He never encouraged Verity's comments and opinions when it came to the practice, and was in no mood to discuss the matter.

'Sharing anything, or anyone, can be a delicate, and often impossible, arrangement,' Verity persisted stoutly. 'I thought Emma was here to help *you*. That fact overcame my prejudice—about which Emma knows—of having a nurse in the first place.'

Simon stiffened; his lips tightened before he replied, 'Emma will still be here to help me when I have the greater need. We shall co-operate. Are you suggesting that we should each have a nurse?'

'Since you've had Emma for the past ten weeks, there might be a great deal in favour of it.' Verity's mood hardened. 'I don't want Emma's attentions to be given solely to the practice,' she said, a sharp note creeping into her voice.

Simon took the cup of tea Emma had poured out for him. He was firm and uncompromising.

'There will be no question of that. Leave me to run the practice, Mother.'

'Now you're cross!' she said petulantly.

'Where did you go this afternoon?' he asked swiftly.

'And don't humour me as though I were an imbecile child,' Verity snapped.

Simon realised that he was on dangerous ground, and that his tactics had been wrong. He hated to admit, even to himself, that the partners had outwitted him over the matter of Emma, but they had right on their side, and there was nothing he could do about it. Emphasis merely put him on the defensive.

Emma said soothingly, 'We went to Cheltenham.'

'Of course, I remember.'

'I walked a little way along the Promenade,' Verity exclaimed, her mood immediately changing. 'And I bought a pair of shoes. My leg didn't seem so stiff.'

'That's splendid,' Simon exclaimed. There was no mistaking the pleasure in his voice.

'Another cup?' Emma asked, looking at him.

'No thank you.' He held her gaze with a disturbing intimacy, and then said almost abruptly, 'You will be wanting to arrange your evening with Stephen.' He gave the matter importance, the words cutting through the emotion previously built up.

Verity was instantly alert. 'An evening with Stephen? When?'

'Nothing is finalised,' Emma broke in swiftly. 'I was going to consult you both first.' She hastened, 'Obviously.'

'I haven't any meetings next week,' Simon said smoothly.

There was nothing in his manner to show that he had the slightest interest in her arrangements with Stephen, other than as any plan might affect the domestic scene.

'Thank you . . . I shall not be going until after I have helped——' Emma looked at Verity as she spoke——'you before dinner, and shall be back to see you to bed.'

'Then,' Simon exclaimed jocularly, 'you will perform miracles.'

'I don't follow.'

'The theatre *and* a meal—in a couple of hours!'

'I shall not go to the theatre,' Emma said coolly.

'That is, of course, up to you. Mrs Jessop——'

'No,' Verity insisted, her expression resistant, 'Odile would help me. She offered only the other day.'

'Then,' Simon retorted, 'you must make your own arrangements.' He smiled, and left them.

Emma felt irritated; she didn't want her time off to be an issue; neither was she flattered by Simon's easygoing acceptance of it, which, she knew, was wholly illogical! Trying to fathom Simon's feelings and reactions was beyond her. She hurried over the thought that she was always endeavouring to read something significant into his words for no better reason than his attraction increased, making it impossible to contemplate him rationally.

'I'm glad you've become friendly with Stephen,' Verity said approvingly. 'He's a most reliable man—charming, too.' She waited for Emma's comment.

'A good friend,' Emma commented pointedly.

'I doubt if that is what is in *his* mind, my dear.'

Was, Emma asked herself, the wish father to the thought? Verity's possessiveness towards Simon manifested itself in so many subtle ways, and Emma knew that, were Simon to suggest taking her, Emma, out alone, Verity's attitude would be very different.

'I've been invited to Odile's on Wednesday,' she said, ignoring Verity's comment. 'But that will not interfere with the routine at all. I haven't seen her cottage yet.'

'You'll love it. Simon spent a great deal of time and money on its conversion. He admires Odile enormously. She's made her own way in the world. Her parents died in a car crash when she was seventeen. It's been a struggle for her.'

Emma dared to suggest, 'Maybe she and Simon will marry one day.'

There was a heavy silence for a second before Verity said with a little secretive smile, 'Odile is certainly the only woman in whom Simon has shown any kind of interest . . . but marriage? I very much doubt it. Simon values his freedom.'

Emma heard the words, realising their gentle irony. Did it never occur to Verity that she, herself, curtailed his freedom in countless ways?

'Ah well,' Emma exclaimed, 'time answers all our questions. Tomorrow is very much an unknown——'

Verity didn't allow Emma to finish the sentence. Her tone was crisp, almost waspish, as she snapped, 'I think I can judge my son better than anyone else. Now I must lie down, Emma.' She glanced at the clock. 'I'm ten minutes late as it is.'

Emma helped her to her room and on to the bed. For the first time since coming to Hunter's Close, faint rebellion surged within her.

Odile, pleasantly and without domination, took over the arranging of Emma's room in the practice quarters, making sensible suggestions and utilising equipment previously discarded in what was termed 'the muddle cupboard'. An attractive 'office' finally emerged, with desk, files, a trolley, dressings, etcetera, until Emma said, 'I shall feel almost like a doctor by the time you've finished!' She was grateful, and surprised, by Odile's enthusiasm.

'Nothing like a place of one's own—quite apart from the fact that it is essential for you if the job's to be done properly.' Odile laughed. 'Method in my madness!'

'Meaning?'

'The work you will spare *me*, to say nothing of the others.'

A little of the gloom that had descended upon Emma lifted; the prospect of no longer working solely for Simon seemed a little less revolutionary. In addition, a rapport had built up between her and Odile, which was encouraging. By Wednesday evening, when Emma arrived at the cottage, all strangeness had gone, and with it her earlier suspicion that Odile might resent her.

The cottage was small, but had a suggestion of space, since two rooms had been knocked into one, with dividing doors that could shut one from the other when convenient. White walls and scarlet furnishings were striking and attractive. 'No pastel shades for me,' Odile announced firmly. 'Sherry, whisky—anything you like.'

'Sherry, please.'

'Dry?'

'Thank you.' As Emma spoke, her gaze fell upon a photograph of Simon which stood on Odile's desk.

'It's good of him, isn't it?' Odile said.

'Very.' The previous bubble of happiness burst. Simon didn't seem the type of man to give a woman his photograph . . . Emma pulled herself up sharply. Again, what did she know of Simon?

'I must admit I more or less demanded it! Verity had insisted on it being taken.' Odile spoke naturally. 'I doubt if Verity knows I have it,' she added. 'She is a very friendly soul, but I often wonder what her attitude would be towards any woman who had designs on Simon!' Odile gave Emma her sherry, took her own, and settled down comfortably in a deep arm-chair opposite Emma. The remark hung between them.

'We shall have to wait and see,' Emma suggested discreetly.

'Your job can't be easy?' Odile looked at Emma with interest. 'I must say you handle her extremely well.'

Emma's reply was honest, 'I haven't been aware of doing so.'

'Simon says you're marvellous.'

Emma gave a little chuckle to cover up the pleasure derived from the statement.

'Praise indeed!' Had she been entirely wrong in her first assessment about Odile's feelings for Simon? Certainly there was nothing self-conscious in Odile's attitude towards him at the moment. Or was the very fact of her bringing his name into the conversation so early on a pointer?

'Yes; Simon doesn't give praise or compliments lightly—which makes both doubly valuable . . .. Are you happy at Hunter's Close?'

'Very.'

'I hope you'll stay.' Odile sipped her sherry and looked at Emma speculatively.

Emma didn't hesitate, 'I can see no reason why I shouldn't do so—unless I fall down on my job.'

'You won't do that . . . but Verity's condition might become extremely taxing, and you're young.'

'The better to cope.'

'But you need some life—and *freedom*.'

'Nurses are not exactly accustomed to freedom,' Emma pointed out.

'True. . . . Shall we eat? It's cold, but I'm starving.' Odile grinned. 'That sounds as though I don't care about you!'

It was an excellent meal of cold chicken, ham, and various salads (not merely the rabbit variety), served with a bottle of white wine and finished with a lemon meringue pie.

'This is Simon's favourite cold meal,' Odile volunteered. 'Plebeian though it is.'

Emma's heart seemed to miss a beat. When had Simon found time to escape for a meal with Odile? On those occasions when he was supposed to be at a hospital committee meeting? She could recall his saying that he would 'eat out', and it had been assumed it would be with fellow members. The expression on Odile's face had changed, Emma realised, becoming dreamy and faraway, as though she were re-living precious moments, lost to everything but their recollection.

Silence fell. They moved from the table and Odile shut the communicating door as they returned to the sitting room which, with the desk lamps lit, looked intimate and attractive.

'I expect you know that Simon originally designed this cottage—you could say he was its architect, and a builder carried out his instructions.'

Emma nodded, trying to sound casual. 'Yes, Verity did mention it.'

Odile smiled, served the coffee and, looking down into her cup and then gazing directly into Emma's eyes, said with faint anxiety, 'Please don't mention

the fact that Simon comes here for a meal sometimes
. . .. As I suggested earlier, there's an uneasy feeling
about Verity's attitude towards any woman in whom
Simon might show an interest. It isn't a question of
secrecy, so much as diplomacy.' The words were
uttered naturally, their confidentiality seeming a
compliment to Emma, who said, feeling suddenly
bleak, 'You can rely on my silence.'

'I know I can . . . it's good to have a colleague—a
woman—to whom one can talk. . . . And now I'd
like to discuss a few points about the practice, and
how we are going to arrange the rota.'

Emma tried to concentrate as Odile outlined several well-thought-out schemes, her ideas practical, but
also imaginative. Emma listened, sometimes without
hearing, as she *felt* Simon's presence in the room.

The telephone ringing interrupted the conversation.

'Here we go,' Odile groaned, then, 'Simon!'

Emma glanced at her wrist-watch, having been
oblivious of time.

Odile said, 'Of course; at once.' She replaced the
receiver, made a wry face and exclaimed, '*Verity* !
Apparently, she thought you would be back at nine-
thirty.' Odile glanced at the clock on the desk. 'And
that's stopped.'

'But Verity told me not to hurry back because
there was something on television she intended to
watch before going to bed,' Emma protested. 'All
the same, I'd no idea it was ten-thirty!'

'At least you are on the spot.' Odile smiled.
'Thank you for coming, Emma. I've enjoyed it.'

'I, too.'

They hurried to the front door.

Simon studied Emma as she stepped into the hall, his expression inscrutable, his attitude distant.

'I'm sorry to be late. I'd no idea of the time.'

'I understood from Verity that you promised to be back at nine-thirty.' He spoke in a matter-of-fact voice.

Emma didn't want to begin any argument by stating, categorically, that he had been misinformed.

'Is she very tired?'

'Agitated.'

'I thought there was a programme she wanted to watch.'

'There was nothing on tonight that appealed to her,' Simon said a trifle wearily. He turned away and disappeared into his study.

Verity was peevish. Why hadn't Emma come back earlier? Her voice went on monotonously and with a precision which often characterises the disease.

Emma made no attempt to defend herself, merely undressed Verity as one might have undressed a rag doll and when, finally, the sheets had been pulled up and smoothed, said, 'Is that better?'

Verity put out her hand.

'You're so good to me . . . I don't know *why* I told Simon you'd promised to be back by nine-thirty.' She looked at Emma pleadingly. 'I seem to want my own way in everything these days.'

'Don't we all?' Emma smiled as she spoke, having no intention of arguing, or attempting to justify herself. 'I should forget about it.'

'I'd love some hot milk,' Verity announced unexpectedly. 'With a little brandy in it.'

'I'll ask Simon for the brandy, and see about the milk myself.'

'Jessop will still be up.' Verity paused. 'Did you enjoy yourself with Odile? What did she talk about?'

'The practice; the future——'

'What future?' It was a faintly alarmed cry.

'The practice future,' Emma said soothingly.

'Not about me?'

'No; not about you ... can't give you *all* the attention, you know.'

'My leg was much less stiff this evening.'

'I'm glad.'

'Didn't you notice when you helped me undress?'

'I noticed you did very little for yourself,' Emma remarked, with a little admonishing nod. 'Now I'll get the milk.'

'And the brandy.'

'And the brandy,' Emma promised, and went from the room, catching Simon as he emerged from his study.

'Verity would like some brandy and milk ... could you give me the brandy, please?' Emma's expression was impassive, her tone formal.

'On one condition,' he exclaimed.

Her eyebrows shot up.

'And that?'

'Come and have a brandy with me after Verity is settled.' He studied her as he spoke, his manner commanding.

'Agreed,' she promised, relenting.

A short while later they settled themselves in their respective chairs in the drawing room.

'Ah!' Simon sighed. It was a relieved, pleasurable

exclamation, as he took the first sip of brandy, looking directly into Emma's eyes, as she also raised her glass. 'It's been a restless evening,' he added.

'Because of Verity?'

'No.' He paused, without taking his gaze from hers. 'Because of you . . . the house is empty when you are not in it.'

Her lips parted; the words shook her. Emotion seemed like a fire within her veins, and she shivered because of the ecstasy his admission awakened. It was useless pretending. Passion flowed between them whenever they were alone together, and excitement mounted even when they were with other people. There was no escaping the desire that overwhelmed them.

The silence of the night isolated them in a moment of complete awareness. Only one lamp glowed in the blue darkness of the room, while, outside, like some enchanted world, the grounds lay beneath the radiance of the moon—mysterious, enticing.

'Shall we go out?' Simon whispered.

Emma was trembling, afraid of his power, his mastery, for, although he asked the question, there was determination in his manner and voice.

'Yes,' she answered tremulously.

But even as they got to their feet, a thud, and Verity's shrill cry, broke the spell and sent them both rushing to her room.

Verity lay on the floor—a pathetic heap—'I reached to turn on the lamp——'

'You have your torch,' Simon exclaimed and stopped, realising that the tension within him was not wholly concern, but frustration.

Emma, deftly, got Verity to her feet and back into

bed, needing only a little help from Simon. Her heart was racing, her senses still tingling with emotion. She avoided Simon's gaze and concentrated solely upon Verity.

'I didn't want a *torch*,' Verity scoffed. 'I wanted the lamp on again, but I lost my balance, and my eyes went all funny.'

Simon murmured a few consoling sympathetic words.

'Where were you both?' Verity asked, faintly suspicious. 'You came very quickly.'

Simon's voice was dangerously patient as he explained, finishing with, 'So you see, you are not the only one who has had some brandy.'

Verity looked from face to face.

'It's late,' she said suddenly, and in a staccato voice, shaking her shoulders like a child as Emma straightened the neck of her nightdress. 'I'm not *hurt* . . . the carpet's thick. Don't *fuss*.'

Simon bit back the words of reproval that rushed to his lips.

Verity, with her familiar gesture, put out her hand and clasped his. 'I really am all right,' she said soothingly. 'Sorry to give you a shock. Now I shan't attempt to read.' She puckered her brows. 'I don't know why I thought I wanted to . . . perhaps I'd dozed off . . . . Thank you, Emma . . . had you finished your brandy?'

'Yes,' Emma said quietly. 'I'm going to bed now.' She looked at Simon—a fleeting glance. 'Goodnight,' she murmured, and went swiftly from the room.

Simon remained standing, dumb, conscious of a great emptiness. The magic had gone.

CHAPTER FOUR

AUTUMN laid golden fingers upon Winchcombe, as it nestled in woodland and valley, burnishing its ancient houses, historic inns, and splendid church. Nearby the ruins of Hayles Abbey kept sentinel, together with the prehistoric Belas Knap. Emma took a deep breath and filled her lungs with the fresh sweet air, as she swung past the gabled, local stone buildings and heard a voice call, 'Emma!' She did not have to turn to know to whom the voice belonged, and Simon caught up with her, saying, 'Where's the fire?'

Happiness touched them suddenly and unexpectedly. They smiled at each other, content to be together.

'I didn't realise I was hurrying,' she exclaimed. 'But I promised Verity I wouldn't be long ... she just wanted a few things from the chemist.' She indicated the parcel she was carrying, and glanced down the hill.

'Time for a coffee!' It was a command, not a question.

'Always time for a coffee.'

Their eyes met; their gaze holding. He guided her into a nearby shop that overlooked the street, and they sat down at a table in the window.

'Dr Conway and his nurse seen together in Winchcombe,' he said with a grin. 'On a morning like this, who cares?'

They looked at each other with eagerness, as though, away from Hunter's Close, responsibility had fallen from their shoulders.

'I like your dress,' he exclaimed irrelevantly. 'That navy-and-white with a touch of yellow——' He smiled wryly, 'My descriptions——' He paused and gave the order for the coffee to the waitress, who recognised him.

'Cakes?' He looked at Emma.

'No thank you.'

'Just two coffees then, please.'

The waitress walked away, thinking that Dr Conway was the most attractive man in the neighbourhood, and that she had never seen him in such good spirits.

'I'd like to forget all about work,' he said abruptly. 'Picnic somewhere. These warm autumn days——' He broke off. 'Why don't we have an evening picnic before this beauty vanishes? Run out somewhere? And let's have red wine—make our own rules!'

Emma's heart quickened its beat. 'At sunset,' she added.

'At sunset,' he echoed. 'Tomorrow.' He might have been looking into her heart as he spoke.

The thought flashed through his mind that he would ask Odile to 'baby-sit' and keep Verity company.

'Tomorrow never comes,' she murmured wistfully.

'Ours will,' he promised, and there was a note of quiet determination in his voice. He added regretfully, 'Now I must get along to see Andrew

Monksford——he's out of hospital after his coronary.'

'And I've a job to do, too,' Emma said. And while they appeared calm, each knew that emotion was building up between them, and that the minutes were full of promise.

They went out to their respective cars. Emma drove back to Hunter's Close, oblivious of her surroundings. The word, '*tomorrow*', sang in her heart, even though her head rejected the possibility of the day-dream being fulfilled.

'You look very happy,' Verity said, conscious of the sparkle in Emma's eyes as she handed over the parcel and enthused, 'It's the most heavenly day. An Indian summer in September is so beautiful. Winchcombe looked golden and——' She stopped, conscious of Verity's inquiring, faintly suspicious, gaze. Trying not to appear flustered, Emma hurried on, 'Now, I must get to work. I've to see Brett's eleven-thirty patient . . . you'll be all right?'

'Perfectly . . . I've had coffee.'

Emma didn't want to be asked for any details of her shopping expedition. It seemed important that Simon's name should not come up at that juncture.

But Verity asked, 'Where's Simon . . . he didn't look in after surgery as he usually does.'

Emma had reached the door, and spoke from there, 'He's in Winchcombe visiting a patient.' With that, she hurried away, changed into her blue dress-cum-overall, and went into the waiting room, calling the patient's name.

Mrs Denby, pale-faced, said, 'I thought I should have to wait a long time.'

'We try to cut waiting to a minimum,' Emma said

pleasantly, and led the way into what was now termed her 'office'. Mrs Denby was a new patient, who had only recently come to live in Winchcombe, and Emma wondered what she would think if she could read her thoughts at that moment and realise that they were bound up entirely with Dr Conway! The efficient nurse image would be transformed into that of a romantic adolescent.

But the moment Emma began to fill in the case history, concentration was immediately restored.

'I—I don't know anything about medicine,' Mrs Denby began half-apologetically.

That, thought Emma, was a refreshing change from the medical-dictionary-fed patients who knew it all, and wanted every symptom listed for perusal. Here was no self-diagnosis to annoy Brett before any examination.

'The cliché that a little knowledge is a dangerous thing,' Emma said with a smile, 'is none the less true. Let me take your blood pressure.'

The systolic pressure was slightly raised; pulse, too. Temperature normal.

Mrs Denby was fifty, thin to the point of emaciation, anxious and apprehensive.

'It's the pain—the indigestion.'

'Hunger pains—gnawing?' Emma prompted.

'That's it. Better when I've had something to eat.'

'Any domestic problems? Anything worrying you?'

Mrs Denby lowered her gaze; confusion crept into her expression, as she said in a breath, 'My daughter ... she's going to have a baby and won't marry the father. What is Dr Curzon like?'

'Very kind,' Emma said reassuringly.

'You see, I've had a lot of the worry. My husband can't cope with problems, and I've spoilt him; I know I have; and *he's* spoilt Enid, our daughter . . . you won't write any of that down, will you?'

'Of course not. This deals with your case notes, not your daughter's. Have you had any previous illnesses, operations?'

'No—just the worry. Jim, my husband, was made redundant last year . . . I won't need an operation—will I?'

Emma said gently, 'I'm not a doctor, Mrs Denby; whatever's wrong with you, Dr Curzon will deal with in the best way possible.'

'Jim couldn't manage on his own; he'd be *lost* without me . . .'

'Let's see if Dr Curzon is free,' Emma said encouragingly, and went into Brett's consulting room.

Brett took the case notes, glanced at them, said, 'Ah!', looked up at Emma and asked, 'Anything else I should know?'

Emma explained about the daughter, and husband, and that the patient knew nothing about medicine.

'Praise the lord!' Brett said heartily. 'Let's have her in . . . thanks, Emma.'

'A pleasure, Dr Curzon,' she retorted breezily.

'You look as though it's spring instead of autumn. Radiant, I believe the word is!'

Emma blushed, smiled, left him, and a few seconds later re-appeared with Mrs Denby.

The next patient, Mrs Gillis, was for Odile, and as Emma went through the routine, she realised how

completely she had shut her mind against Odile's
confidence the night she visited the cottage. The idea
of building up the relationship between Simon and
Odile, indulging in suspicion and destructive jealousy, was not in her nature. Also, to allow Simon to
become an issue between her and Odile would,
Emma knew, have destroyed not only the harmony
within the practice, but outside it, as well.

'What face is Mrs Gillis wearing today?' Odile
asked wryly, as Emma handed her the notes.

'Her, "I *look* well, but I'm so *ill*"!'

Odile made a despairing gesture. Mrs Gillis was
an hysteric whom Odile tolerated for the sake of the
husband and family.

'Have we got the X-rays from Owen?'

'Yes; on your desk.'

Odile studied them, and the report.

'All this should convince even Paula Gillis! We've
gone over her with a tooth-comb. She hasn't a thing
wrong with her.'

'You really care about that family—don't you?'

'Yes; Ralph Gillis is a fine man—Simon's patient
and friend—and there are two delightful boys. No
worries of any kind, and yet Paula Gillis ruins
everything by her selfish behaviour. I've tried, God
knows . . . bring her in, and give me patience!'

Emma felt that her feet hardly touched the ground
for the rest of the day and when she, Simon and
Verity were seated at the dinner table, she was afraid
that her bubbling happiness must be obvious, for
Verity intercepted every glance she and Simon exchanged.

Simon broke a somewhat awkward silence with,

'I want you to come over to Painswick with me to-morrow evening, Emma. I'm standing in for Miles Risedale, a colleague.'

'What time in the evening?' Verity asked severely.

'Sixish.'

'Oh, so it won't interfere with dinner.'

'I'm not certain of my movements, Mother, and have asked Odile to keep you company in our absence.' Simon's voice was kindly, but firm.

'You mean you and Emma are going *out* to dinner?'

'Possibly. Jessop has his orders, and if we should need anything on our return, it will be available.'

Verity's back seemed to stiffen. Her mood was hostile and truculent.

'I hate anything to spoil the evenings. Why——'

Simon cut in with authority, 'You'll have Odile with you. I cannot be tied.'

'Why do you need Emma?' Verity was not going to be silenced.

'Because, unfortunately, the patient is alone, and she will welcome the presence of a nurse.'

'Don't tell me she needs a *chaperone*.'

'No; but I do,' he retorted, introducing a lighter note, hoping to forestall further questioning.

The thought flashed through Emma's mind that she was very grateful Simon owned the house, and therefore could speak from strength instead of as a man living with his mother. It seemed suddenly to be of vital importance, and gave Emma a sense of relief. The fact that Verity's apartments were self-contained, and on the ground floor, lent a feeling of detachment, almost as though Verity was isolated from the heart of it all.

'And *I* need Emma,' Verity insisted.

Simon forced a smile and turned to Emma, 'See how important you have become.' He added swiftly, 'Brett and Stephen will take surgery.'

'You're very thoughtless and—and *hard*,' Verity said shakenly.

The words came like thunder, and while Emma felt a natural pity for Verity, she resented the grossly unfair remark, considering that, if anything, Simon pandered to his mother, rather than neglected her. That, however, in the circumstances, she understood, and excused, because, even in the short while she herself had been at Hunter's Close, she had emulated him.

Simon knew that only silence could deal with the situation. He made no attempt to justify himself. But a little later, said, 'Now if you'll excuse me, I've some paper-work to do.'

'Can it wait until after coffee?' Verity protested.

Simon sighed inwardly, but said, 'Very well.' He moved to Verity's chair and helped her to her feet.

'Thank you,' Verity smiled sweetly. 'I do like our evenings to be undisturbed. And it's such a beautiful evening, too. Far warmer than in the summer . . . have you ever been to Painswick, Emma?'

'No,' said Emma, not daring to look at Simon.

'It's known as "The Queen of the Cotswolds" and its clipped yews are marvellous . . . I believe there are about ninety or so; some, two hundred years old.' She gave a little sigh. 'I used to go up Painswick Beacon. Wonderful views.'

Emma knew that those last words were the

most telling of all.

Jessop brought the coffee and Emma did her best to pour it out. Her hands were shaking, her heart thumping.

The telephone ringing relieved the tension and Simon answered it thankfully.

'Mrs Newton . . . your husband. Of course, I'll come at once.'

'I'll get your bag,' Emma said immediately, hurrying to his consulting room and then joining him at the front door.

'Sometimes fate conspires *with* us,' he said. 'Painswick is genuine, and we can snatch an hour afterwards.' Their hands touched as Emma gave him the bag; eyes met eyes in understanding, before the car raced away.

'Always emergencies,' Verity protested as Emma re-joined her. 'Where has he gone this time?'

'To Charlton Abbots.'

'At least that's near. Do you know the patient?'

Emma avoided going into details of what was a distressing bronchial asthma case, and conveniently remembered a memo she wanted to leave for Odile. At that moment, being with Verity was claustrophobic, almost as though the drawing-room walls were closing in. She escaped to Odile's consulting room, wrote the memo, and placed it on Odile's desk. Only tomorrow was important, and she stood for a minute day-dreaming. Footsteps along the corridor set her nerves tingling, but in a matter of seconds Odile came unexpectedly into the room.

'So it's you,' Odile cried. 'I saw the light fanning out from the door . . . something wrong?'

Emma explained, indicating the memo slip.

Odile glanced at it and nodded. 'I came over for some notes I need for my thesis ... Simon not about?'

'He's at Charlton Abbots.'

'Oh, that means poor Mr Newton ... did Simon mention that I'm going to baby-sit tomorrow evening?'

'Yes; it's good of you.'

'Anything to help. Simon's pretty tense at the moment, and that means Verity's being difficult, which can't be easy for you.' Odile studied Emma reflectively. 'At least everything is going smoothly in the practice ... you are an enormous help, you know.' She added, 'And you're happy?'

'Very happy.'

'I must say, you look it ... ah well, goodnight, Emma. Thanks for the memo. I'll make sure to get in touch with Mrs Mornay before we begin surgery.' Odile stood still, a faraway look in her eyes. 'Strange,' she said, 'how empty this practice part can seem when there's no work going on.' With that she hurried towards the door and left. Emma remained alone for a few seconds, feeling as she had done on that first evening when she had seen Odile looking across the room at Simon. . . .

When it was time for Simon and Emma to leave the following evening, Verity insisted, 'You could surely be back for dinner at seven-thirty ... we'll wait for you.'

'Please, Mother.' Simon tried to be patient. 'Emma's done everything necessary for you, and

Odile will be with you in a matter of minutes. She'll stay until we return.'

'Will you call on the Willis's? They're near Painswick.'

'I doubt it.' Simon spoke pleasantly, smiled, said goodbye, and almost propelled Emma from the room.

'We might be going around the world,' he exclaimed, as he and Emma settled themselves in the car. He glanced at her as he drove swiftly down the drive. There was an intimacy between them as the mood of yesterday returned and, with it, an acute awareness that they were out alone together, escaping from surveillance and rigid routine.

'I don't know this patient, Mrs Clarence,' Simon said, 'but I bless her. From what I can gather, she lives alone. Miles Risedale's secretary couldn't throw much light on the case, but Miles had left it that I should be contacted in the event of Mrs Clarence needing any attention. I don't think Miles's name will mean anything to you.'

Emma could hardly say that nothing meant anything to her, except that she was sitting there beside him excited, heart racing.

'No, I can't remember hearing of a Miles Risedale.'

'We stand in for each other from time to time . . . I mustn't forget to call you *Nurse*!'

'Of course, *Dr Conway* . . . do you really need me?'

The words hung between them, their meaning rushing entirely out of context as he said, 'Oh, yes; I need you, Emma.' His voice was low, and drew her into his world.

'Professionally,' she added.

'Professionally, too. Miles has a habit of handing over the unusual ones to me! And I don't have to tell you there are quite a number of women patients that I would never dream of examining without a third person present.'

Emma studied him, aware of his strength and the purposefulness of his finely etched features. The attraction was sharp and physical. Emotion rushed up between them. 'Are we nearly there?' she asked tensely.

Painswick was on the main road from Cheltenham to Stroud, and Simon said, 'The house is near the church apparently, and we turn off here.'

Within a short while they were standing at the door of what was an attractive cottage.

A woman in her early thirties—dark-haired, striking—answered their ring, and almost collapsed into their arms.

'So giddy . . . faint.'

They got her into a sitting room and on to a sofa.

'So—sorry.' Grey eyes met Emma's, and relief showed in them.

Simon put his fingers on her pulse, and then took her blood pressure. She was gradually recovering, the colour returning to her cheeks. Simon talked quietly, questioning with gentle persuasion.

'Now I want to examine you, Mrs Clarence. Nurse Reade will see you upstairs and help you undress. I'll wait down here until you are ready.'

Consternation showed immediately in the now half-frightened eyes. 'But——'

'You sent for me,' Simon said firmly, 'and you are not well.'

'I panicked yesterday; but I didn't make it an emergency ... I mean, I've been feeling faint and nauseated ... I thought you'd prescribe something——'

Simon's expression was half-smiling and half-warning. 'I don't treat symptoms, Mrs Clarence. And neither does my colleague, Dr Risedale.'

'No; no, of course not.'

Emma took Mrs Clarence's arm and they went upstairs together.

A few minutes later Simon joined them and made a thorough examination, although it did not require any great diagnostic ability to know that Mrs Clarence was pregnant. On being told, she gave a horrified gasp, protested that it was not possible, and then, later, confided that her husband had been away in the Middle East for a year, and was returning at the end of the month. There was anguish in her expression.

In that moment Rita Clarence looked more like a pathetic school-girl than a mature woman. There was a silent pleading of 'Help me', as she looked at Simon and asked, 'Are you *sure*?'

'As sure as you are,' he said gently. 'You dreaded, and yet wanted, confirmation. Nothing is as bad as it seems once you have faced up to it, and come to a decision.'

There was a moment's painful silence, then she said honestly, 'I'd love a child.' A glimmer of hope pierced the darkness of fear. 'You see, I really love my husband, but he will never forgive me—never.'

She spoke as though praying to be contradicted.

'You cannot know that until you've asked to *be* forgiven.'

'Would *you* forgive your wife?' The question tumbled out in relief at being able to discuss the problem.

Simon stiffened slightly, resisting any intrusion into his emotional life.

'I'd like to think I would,' he answered.

She said quietly, 'You've been so kind—thank you for coming. Uncertainty, desperation, increase with loneliness.'

'Could you get away for a week or two—go to friends?' Simon suggested.

'I shall go to my sister. She's wise and understanding. Now that I'm certain . . .'

'And you *must* have ante-natal care,' Simon insisted.

'Would you do something for me?'

'If it is possible—certainly.'

'Then tell Dr Risedale all the facts. You see, he knows my husband and, well——'

'Doctors are not judges, Mrs Clarence, but if that is your wish, and I have your permission—I'll do so. You couldn't be in better hands.'

'I realise that. And I like and respect him.' She paused, then, 'I feel better now—much better. You've helped me more than you know.'

'And don't forget that I'm here if there's anything I can do before Dr Risedale returns——'

'Thank you; I won't forget.'

'And now have a rest; the symptoms will pass, and when the tension lessens you will feel better in any case.' Simon held out his hand and shook hers. 'You've courage—draw on it.'

'I will . . . and thank your nurse. She, too, was so kind.' Emma had waited in the car during the conversation.

Simon left the cottage and joined Emma, sliding into the driving seat and not speaking until they had reached the road.

'This is where everything to do with our profession ends,' he said, relaxing.

Emma was hardly conscious of the short journey through leafy lanes until they finally reached the summit of a steep hill, which might have been the top of the world, with its illimitable views—deep valleys and, in the far distance, the purple smudge of the Welsh mountains.

'This is my miniature Harefield Beacon—a beauty spot which we haven't time to reach tonight.' Simon looked into her eyes. 'The sun is beginning to set.' He helped her from the car and collected a thick rug and picnic basket from the boot, choosing a spot where they could spread out comfortably. Above them the sky was an explosion of colour that dyed the landscape.

A soft breeze faintly ruffled Emma's hair as she sat there, watching him uncork the wine. Emotion, a little shyness, touched her as awareness of him became exciting and acute.

He handed her the glass. 'A glass of wine, and thou,' he quoted.

They drank together, their gaze holding.

'Freedom,' he murmured. 'All this—*ours*. You look so beautiful as you sit there, the rays of the sun on your hair. Oh, Emma; I've dreamed of a moment like this.'

Wonderment was in her eyes as she whispered, 'So have I.'

He took the glass from her hand and put it aside with his own and then, masterfully, drew her into his arms, feeling her body curve against his as his lips parted hers, and ecstasy flowed over them like a warm sensuous tide. His kiss was passionate and demanding, his touch, rapture. Her head was cradled on his shoulder and he looked down at her as she drew back, breathless. 'Is this a prelude?' he asked hoarsely, his mouth closing over hers again, his arms holding her in a vice-like grip.

Every nerve in her body responded to his touch, until at last, exhausted, she sat upright, but without removing her gaze from his.

'A prelude,' she said in a breath, her heart thudding wildly. 'I like that: it gives us another tomorrow.' She knew instinctively that his sensitivity would match her own, and emotion tore at her, sending her once more into his arms.

They stayed there, ecstasy merging with discovery as, finally, he let her go, his release a concession to a greater fulfilment that was inevitable. The dusk was gathering around them.

Simon handed back her glass and raised his own. They drank, silently. And her heart was whispering, 'This is Simon—*Simon* sitting here beside you.' The world had become enchanted.

He leaned towards her and grasped her hand, raising it to his lips. 'I dare not kiss you again,' he said. 'Not here—now. We've got to get back very soon——'

She lowered her gaze for a second. She knew that neither could endure Verity's suspicious probing inquiries.

'It's been perfect,' Emma said shakily, glancing around her. And now the tang of autumn touched them; the great mural of the sky was hazy, as though smoke had softened its brilliant hue, turning it to pastel shades that shimmered in the last light.

'And I must take you home,' Simon said firmly. 'It is getting cold.'

Emma shivered—but with emotion.

They drove back through the gathering darkness, and although they were silent, the words were there in the deep emotion that flowed between them. And as they finally got out of the car and faced each other, the look they exchanged was full of promise and desire.

'Go in,' Simon said, 'I'll join you after I've spoken to Jessop.'

It was the first time Emma had realised they had not touched the delicacies prepared for them.

Verity was in a good mood. Odile's company had pleased her.

'We've been talking about this house,' Verity said eagerly. 'Odile loves it, too.' She spoke like a child thrilled by someone appraising a toy.

'I can't imagine your ever leaving it,' Odile said conversationally, addressing Simon.

Both he and Emma were now seated in their respective chairs, trying to behave with naturalness.

'That,' cried Verity emphatically, 'is the last thing.'

To Simon and Emma the scene was an anti-climax. They were in no mood for aimless conversation and were infinitely grateful when Odile, sensing Verity's tiredness, said she must leave.

'Simon will see you to the cottage,' Verity announced, 'while Emma's getting me to bed.'

Emma longed to escape. She had been left on the edge of fulfilment. Simon's kiss lingered in her memory; the memory of the evening seeming part of a dream. A prelude.

She attended to Verity who said, 'I'm so *sleepy* tonight; I don't know why. Odile is very entertaining, but talking tires me.' She looked at Emma searchingly. 'You haven't said anything about your evening . . . what was the patient like?'

'Pleasant.'

'*Pleasant*,' Verity echoed critically, 'I hate that word. But, then, there are a great many things I hate these days that I used not to hate. You look absent-minded.'

Emma kept her nerve, smiled, smoothed the sheets and bent and kissed Verity's forehead.

Verity said abruptly, 'I expect Simon will stay and have a drink with Odile . . . Goodnight. I don't want the light left on—too tired.'

Emma left the darkened room, her thoughts chaotic. Would Simon stay to have a drink? She ached for him to return, and stood in the hall, tense and listening for every sound that might herald his footsteps. But after a few seconds she began to mount the stairs, disappointment, and a sense of loss, overwhelming her.

Suddenly, unexpectedly, she heard her name

called softly and, looking up, saw Simon standing on the landing—a tall imposing figure in a silk, deep burgundy dressing gown that enhanced his attractiveness and masculinity.

She reached him quickly with a little cry of delight.

'I waited up here for you,' he said significantly, putting an arm around her waist as they moved slowly towards her bedroom. There they paused, eyes meeting, then wordlessly, went into the moonlit darkness, closing the door behind them.

Every nerve in her body was quivering, her heart racing, as she asked herself if this was really happening. But Simon was there, beginning to undress her, until at last she felt the warmth and power of his strong limbs against hers, as his hands caressed her and his lips found hers.

'Emma,' he whispered passionately. '*My darling.*'

He held her with such possessiveness that her body seemed to melt into his, the touch of flesh against flesh flooding them with desire, as her arms reached up and encircled his neck, drawing him ever closer, their need for each other wiping out time and place until they became part of the night and the moonlight. His strength thrilled and dominated her so that pain became rapture until, at last, passion spent, she lay quietly in his arms, her eyes meeting his with a radiance that answered his mute enquiry. And now he held her with tenderness and protection, and she buried her face in his shoulder, whispering his name, overcome by the wonder of belonging to him.

They slept in each other's arms, and after an hour or so, she awakened and immediately he stirred, knowing with a pang that he must go. His kiss was lingering, and Emma clung to him. He murmured her name and went swiftly and silently from the room.

She lay there and, gradually, ecstasy became blurred by reality that crept up like a dark, menacing shadow. He had made love to her, but at no time had he told her he loved her, or mentioned the word. And she knew, with devastating certainty, that she was in love with him, and had been since that first night at Hunter's Close.

CHAPTER FIVE

EMMA met Simon the following morning in a mood of shyness and anticipation. Would he mention the previous night; enlarge on his feelings? But he rushed towards her, saying, 'I'm going to the Gillis's. Looks as though Ralph's having a coronary. Carry on with surgery if I'm not back.' With that he was out of the house, seeming to take off in his car.

Jessop hovered. 'That means no breakfast, Nurse.'

Emma looked dazed as she sat down at the table. Food was the last thing she wanted, but she knew it wouldn't help if she fainted through hunger and emotion. Ralph Gillis! The last person; and yet what man wouldn't ultimately be the victim of his wife's hypochondria, after years of stress and strain, pandering to her idiosyncracies?

Odile appeared. 'I had an early call and wondered

if there was any coffee about,' she said with a smile. 'There's half an hour before surgery ... where's Simon?'

Emma told her, and she gave a little gasp of dismay, then, 'Pity it isn't his wife,' she exclaimed bluntly.

Everything, Emma thought, seemed so normal, while she felt that she was watching herself putting on an act, playing the part assigned to her.

'It's going to be one of those days,' Odile warned. 'At least,' she added, 'Simon wasn't called out in the night. And that all sounds a bit Irish.' She poured out her coffee from the pot Emma indicated. 'Simon had obviously not had breakfast,' Odile added.

'No.'

'And you don't look exactly enamoured with yours!'

Emma started, flushed slightly, and hastened, 'Odile, I'm so *sorry* I didn't suggest breakfast for you. I'll ring and——'

Odile grinned. 'Not to worry; I'd have asked for something ... don't you feel too good?'

Emma's voice was convincing as she said, 'I'm fine. I haven't quite got used to illness, and possible death, in the dining room as it were. Everything is so different in hospital.'

The explanation satisfied Odile, who nodded her understanding.

'Verity was in good form last evening, by the way ... talked to me of her school days, and of your parents.'

Emma felt a guilty pang. Momentarily, they had dropped out of her world. She put aside her plate, and turned her chair away from the table, leaving only her coffee which she proceeded to drink.

'I must write to my parents,' she murmured, listening, she knew foolishly, for the sound of Simon's car. He could not possibly be back so soon, even though the Gillis's lived in Winchcombe. Words had no meaning just then, because she could not collect her thoughts, or control the emotion that was like hunger in her heart. Odile might not have heard her. She was looking out over the grounds, which lay green and gold in the morning light. The fresh pungent smell of chrysanthemums, dew-drenched, hung in the crisp air. The sun touched the tips of firs, beeches, and the dark majestic beauty of cedars.

'I don't feel like work today,' she exclaimed. 'At least I'm not on surgery this morning. I get restless in the autumn ... I'd like something exciting to happen.' She paused. 'That's Simon——'

Emma got swiftly to her feet, and she and Odile hurried out into the hall as Simon entered it. One look at his face told them the dread news.

'There was nothing I could do ... he died almost as I got there ... a massive coronary.'

'Oh, no!' Emma cried.

'What about *her*?' Odile asked, a trifle belligerently.

'Hysterical. I've sedated her. Fortunately, the sister-in-law is staying there, so someone will be in charge.' Simon made a hopeless gesture, avoiding Emma's gaze. 'He was a fine man and my friend.'

'Come and have a coffee,' Odile said gently, touching his arm, and urging him into the dining room.

A bleak sensation of helplessness and inadequacy washed over Emma. In that moment she felt that her absence would not be noticed, and she went along to Verity's room.

It was not until just before surgery that she saw Simon again, when the partners gathered in the common room. He looked like a man in a trance, and there was a hush over the practice as he said, addressing Emma, 'Mrs Morris is coming to see me early this morning. Check her prescriptions and make a careful note of her blood pressure . . . what's the waiting room like?'

'Filling up,' Emma said, trying to make her voice sound natural.

'Good; I want to be kept busy.' He looked from face to face. 'I'll take any extra load today.' With that he walked away, adding, 'Time we started.'

Stephen exclaimed, 'Simon brings a shutter down when he's upset. He and Ralph were close.'

Brett nodded his agreement, while Odile stood silently sympathetic. Then she said, 'I'm going to start my rounds. Simon will work himself to a standstill. I know him.' She shook her head and went from the room.

Maude appeared in the doorway. 'Your first patient's here, Dr Stephen.'

'Coming.' He glanced at Emma. 'I'd like a word with you later on.'

'Make it immediately after surgery. I've a lot to do for Verity today—she wants to go shopping.' Emma's voice was flat.

'I'll try,' Stephen said.

Emma went into the waiting room and summoned

Mrs Morris, took her into the office, checked as Simon had indicated, and then went along to his consulting room. He was standing looking out of the window, and turned as she entered. There was nothing in his expression, his attitude, to suggest that her presence meant anything to him. Was it possible, she reflected, that she had lain in his arms the previous night, or was it the figment of her imagination? It was as though some unseen force was tearing her apart, while she looked at him, telling herself that, obviously, making love had merely been an incident to him, whereas, to her, it had been a commitment. For a second their eyes met, but it was impossible to fathom his thoughts. Was this the reaction from Ralph Gillis's death? Did that wipe out all other considerations? Or was he regretting his own folly and criticising her for her part in it? His words, '*Emma . . . my darling*', echoed hauntingly. And yet . . . was she building it up out of all proportion? She had no precedent by which to judge either his behaviour, or her own. Just because she was in love with him, did not mean that he should become the romantic lover. Pride helped her to regain composure as she said in a matter-of-fact voice, 'Mrs Morris is here . . . are you ready for her now?'

It seemed that he stiffened slightly as he said, 'Yes . . . thank you,' he added with his accustomed courtesy.

'Oh . . .' Emma paused in the doorway. 'Verity wants me to take her shopping after surgery. Will that be in order?'

'Of course.'

Emma fetched Mrs Morris and escaped. She was

shaking, her legs feeling like putty. She wanted the luxury of tears because the pain, the hurt, was deep and inescapable. She felt rejected, stunned.

Stephen appeared in her office as the surgery doors shut.

'I want you to meet my parents,' he said unexpectedly. 'How about lunch on Sunday? Brett will be on call. I'm not going to allow any excuses.'

'I wasn't,' Emma said, forcing a little laugh, 'going to make any.' At that moment the invitation seemed like a bonus, giving her a means of escape from Hunter's Close on a day when Simon tried to be at home as much as possible. She added, 'I'd very much like to meet your parents.'

He looked pleased. His feelings for Emma had deepened over the past weeks and he wanted to establish priority.

'Splendid . . . you can't be on duty all the time.' There was a trace of belligerence in his tone.

'I'm not expected to be,' she flashed back at him.

'Sometimes it seems like it,' he countered.

'Things are not always what they seem.' She stopped abruptly, the unreality of the scene and the conversation, striking a hideously false note. Here she was, arranging to meet Stephen's parents, when every thought and longing embraced Simon. But, she told herself, the last thing she intended was to allow Simon to sense her disillusionment, or to imagine that her happiness rested solely in his hands. Her thoughts swung about like a feather in the wind. Suppose she was misjudging him? The death of a friend might surely be justification for preoccupation and the shelving of purely personal considerations.

Dinner that evening was a strained, silent affair. Verity kept up a running commentary about the morning's shopping, breaking off at one point to say to Simon, 'I *know* you and Ralph were good friends, but I'm sure *he* would not have wished you to be so gloomy. Don't you agree with me, Emma?'

'I'm sorry,' Simon said tersely, 'to be a wet blanket; but I can't indulge in trivia at the moment. We've finished, haven't we?' He looked from face to face, his expression inscrutable.

When they reached the drawing room and were drinking their coffee, he addressed Emma suddenly, 'I hear you are to meet Stephen's parents on Sunday.' He made it sound a momentous issue.

There was a tense silence. Emma had intended mentioning the invitation a little later on.

'News travels fast,' she said.

'Stephen mentioned it. Did you regard it as a secret to be divulged at a specific time?' His gaze was steely and uncompromising.

'Of course not ... this evening has hardly provided the right climate in which to discuss what you might call "trivia".' Inwardly, she seethed. 'If it is not convenient for me to go out on Sunday, then——'

'That doesn't come into it,' he interrupted, his voice impatient.

'Then what does?' Verity asked innocently. 'Emma doesn't want to be stuck here with us every weekend.' She smiled at Emma. 'You will like the senior Gilmores; they're young and modern. In Hugh and Clare's category. Stephen's a favourite of mine. Understanding man.'

'Why not write him a testimonial?' Simon suggested.

Verity stared at Simon critically, her mood, fortunately, not aggressive. 'I would if he needed one.'

Simon put down his coffee cup. 'If you'll excuse me, I'm going for a walk.'

Verity said, almost as though soothing a child, 'Why not go and have a drink with Odile? She always cheers you up.'

Simon hesitated, frowned, and then exclaimed, 'A good idea.'

Emma sat there, feeling that she was dying a little, as her heart-beats seemed to choke her .... *Last* evening. It wasn't possible that life could change so drastically in twenty-four hours.

'Don't take too much notice of Simon,' Verity said knowingly, after he had left them, 'he reacts like this to personal sorrow. Odile knows how to handle him.'

Emma felt a pang. Not of jealousy, but confusion and misery. Was she being unreasonable? Yet, a look, a word, or the touch of his hand, would have meant happiness and security. Even their earlier intimacy—when a glance had silently conveyed their attraction—had vanished. Simon might have been a stranger whom she had met for the first time without interest, or possible involvement. '*Odile knows how to handle him*'. The sentence was like an indictment, emphasising that she did not. The possibility struck her that Odile might be more to him than just a friend. Odile, after all, was charming and sophisticated. By comparison she, herself, slid into insignificance, disgusted by her own reactions. Until the previous night, she had lived with hope and excitement; now there was only baffled uncertainty, coupled with humiliation, because no matter what the circumstances, or Simon's attitude, she loved him, and could not envisage life without him.

During the next few days the practice was stretched to its limit, with early autumn viruses, illness among the elderly, midders that developed complications, so that patients seemed to be moving on a conveyor belt, with home visits doubled and surgeries full. There was no time for pleasantries, brief gatherings for coffee, or comments outside the sphere of medicine. Emma played her role of the efficient nurse, silently, and without complaint at being overworked. Verity's leg seemed stronger, but her temper was frayed because she missed Emma's constant ministrations, and she protested violently to Simon, on the one evening he had managed to salvage an hour.

'Emma came to help *me*—that was to be the first consideration. But all you care about is the wretched practice and the patients.'

'The patients *are* my practice,' Simon insisted.

'You think far more about them than you do me—give them far more attention. Besides, what about Emma?' The atmosphere became electric. 'If you think,' Verity rushed on, 'that Emma enjoys being at work all the hours there are, then——'

'Has Emma complained?' Simon asked curtly, almost as though Emma wasn't there.

'No, but——'

Emma cut in, 'There is no question of complaint.'

She paused and added coldly, 'Were that so, I should say so, and think in terms of finding another job.' The words were out before she had time to calculate their effect, or implication.

'I see.' He looked at her long and hard. 'In that case we know where we stand,' he said icily. 'I just don't pretend to understand you these days.'

'Nor I you,' she flashed back, her nerves raw, control ebbing. 'Everyone has been working as hard as humanly possible, and no one has asked for any quarter.' Fury mingled with desire in an explosion of emotion. She could never forget the fact that this man had made love to her. He looked handsome, commanding and challenging, as he stood there, and she ached to be in his arms while contemptuous of her own weakness.

'You *know* how much I appreciate the fact,' he said.

Verity had shrunk back in her chair, Emma's words about leaving coming as a shock.

'You—you wouldn't *leave* me,' she gasped. 'Emma——' her voice rose shrilly, 'you *wouldn't*?'

The room was suddenly filled with a silence that seemed to be waiting for some catastrophic happening. Emma turned away from Simon and moved to Verity's side. 'No,' she said solemnly, 'I wouldn't leave you—not just now, anyway.'

Verity was mollified, but not satisfied. She didn't understand why Simon and Emma should be so angry with each other. Yet, if she were honest, the fact didn't wholly displease her. She did not want Simon to become involved with Emma, because that would give Emma control and power. All she asked was that they should be pleasant and impersonal and, she told herself comfortingly, she always managed to have her own way. At the moment she would not worry about tomorrow. . . .

'A reprieve, you see, Mother,' Simon said. 'We must be grateful.' Then, as if his own words offended him by introducing what could seem to be a sarcastic note, he added swiftly, 'I'm glad.'

Emma was trembling as he went from the room, revolt consuming her. Revolt against him and against herself. Her head swirled with tormenting thoughts, fragments of conversation, memories of ecstasy.

The front door opened and closed somewhat noisily. The house became still—and empty. . . .

When Sunday arrived, Emma regretted what she now realised had been a precipitate act in agreeing to have lunch with Stephen and his parents. She had, in effect, succumbed to the cardinal error in a woman's make-up—that of rushing in the opposite direction when faced with rejection. And when Simon appeared to ignore her, Stephen had boosted her ego by inviting her to meet his parents. Now she could neither cancel the appointment, nor denigrate that invitation by admitting her reason for acceptance.

She did not see Simon until she was about to leave the house. He had breakfasted late, and arranged to do two visits during the morning. His car drew up in the drive as she was about to get into hers.

He looked at her impassively. 'Good morning— and it is one,' he added, holding open her car door as she got into the driving seat.

'Actually,' she said, far too brightly, 'it is after-noon, but I agree with you: it is beautiful.' *We're talking about the weather,* her thoughts raced. 'I shall be back immediately after lunch,' she said.

'Better not to make any promises,' he suggested.

'A philosophy of yours,' she countered im-mediately, and seeing the look of puzzlement on his face, hastened, 'with which I heartily agree.' She switched on the engine. 'But I shall still be back after lunch. Verity may want to go for a run.'

Simon continued to study Emma in faint be-wilderment, then stepped back in what seemed a gesture of dismissal. 'Enjoy yourself!'

'*Enjoy yourself!*' The words echoed in her ears. No doubt he actually believed she would, too! Emotion quickened her heart-beat. *Simon!* If only she could forget him; pretend that he was the last man on earth she could ever love. She jammed her foot down on the accelerator, the bronzed landscape rushing by. After a few deep breaths, however, she relaxed and stopped breaking the speed limit. A pang shot through her; a sick regret. These days could have been so wonderful . . . if only he could have loved her. She wanted to cry; to stop being proud and stoical. As it was, the Gilmore house came into view—a Georgian dwelling that stood only a few yards from the road. Emma glanced at herself in the driving mirror, changed her expression, and emerged from the car looking a happy young girl whose heart just happened to feel like lead.

But there she paused and looked around her. The countryside was an autumn tapestry set against misty blue. The smell of bonfires wafted in the cool noon air. In the distance Bredon Hill rose against the sky, gentle, a landmark for miles, its varied hues of purple, green and gold softened with shadows cast by the sun. She thought poignantly that, without happiness, looking at beauty was like seeking a reflection in fog.

Stephen came out of the house, buoyant, welcoming; his sophisticated air vanishing. In that second Emma realised, with a shock, that he was in love with her. Now that she was in love herself, it was easy to recognise the symptoms in someone else.

'Thanks be,' he said in greeting. 'I was afraid you might not be able to get away.'

'A quiet morning,' she said, a trifle nervously.

Stephen's parents, Keith and Joan, were friendly people who loved their home, country life, and simplicity. Emma felt, rightly, that they asked for nothing more than that Stephen should find the right wife, be happy, have children, so that they, in turn, could enjoy grandchildren. Emma knew that she was being assessed hopefully. It made her feel that she was there under false pretences, which she hated, finding it impossible to be natural. All she could think of was Simon; hearing his voice, the words he had uttered to her; the looks they had exchanged. Even the countryside breathed his name, and she saw his face in the huge log fire that burned in the chintzy drawing room where they gathered for pre-lunch drinks. She wondered, as they all sat talking about everything and nothing, what the Gilmores would think about her relationship with Simon? Stephen was attentive, faintly possessive, and wholly at ease in his environment. Could she have been there with Simon, identified with him, *belonging*, it would all have been perfect. As it was, she found herself retreating from personal questions, her thoughts scuttling to find innocuous topics which petered out and led to awkward pauses, when the silence seemed noisy.

Yet, Emma reflected, this was the kind of friendly informal atmosphere that appealed to her, and Stephen was a man easy to love—natural, sympathetic, understanding, whose broad shoulders were made to take the burdens of other people. He met her gaze, but she looked away because her heart had nothing to say to him. A little later, after a typical Sunday lunch, perfectly cooked, he said, 'How about a walk, Emma? Do you fancy a climb to Langley Hill?'

'I must get back.' It was then ten minutes to three. She was half-apologetic. 'I know you understand.' She looked at Joan Gilmore as she spoke, then glanced at Keith and, finally, to Stephen. 'Verity may want to go out, and——'

'Then let Simon take her,' Stephen said. 'Anyway, let's have a short walk—even if only in the garden.'

'I wanted to talk to you,' he insisted, once they were out of the house. 'I'm in love with you, Emma—you know that, don't you?'

'Not until today,' she replied honestly.

'And I want to marry you,' he added a trifle fiercely. 'There are no problems. My parents don't expect me to spend my life here, with them, and we can buy a house wherever you like.' He moved close to her. 'Emma——'

She stepped back, almost as though warding him off, as she said urgently, 'No, Stephen ... I'm honoured, but——'

'You're not involved with someone else?' There was a pained expression on his face.

'No, nothing like that.' How bitter those words seemed.

'Then it's up to me to change your mind.' There was a finality in the utterance.

'But——'

'I've plenty of patience,' he insisted. 'For the moment it's enough that you know how I feel.' He added, 'And I rather think your parents would approve of me. At least I've met them.'

'No one,' Emma said gently, 'could disapprove.'

'Provided you don't tell me that you're fond of me,' he rushed on, 'then we'll say no more about it. At least I'm on the spot, and can keep my eye on you.'

'With pleasure,' she retorted, trying to sound bright.

She drove back to Hunter's Close in confusion, not wanting the complication of Stephen's love for her, and wishing desperately that she could marry him. It would be so simple. They had everything in common, and no relatives to interfere. He was a doctor, too, so she would not be leaving behind the world of medicine which was an integral part of her life. A little flicker of hope touched her. Suppose her feelings for Simon were, after all, nothing more than infatuation? Their relationship a folly she regretted. Stephen was everything any woman could desire in a man. For a second the day looked brighter, the pain seemed less acute. And then, as she reached the drive of Hunter's Close and was about to get out of the car, Simon appeared in the doorway of the house and stepped forward. At the sight of him emotion struck with a passionate intensity, her heart quickened its beat almost as though he had touched it with some invisible ray. There was a power about him that manifested itself even in the most commonplace situation; his personality making it impossible to ignore, or be indifferent to, him.

'Hello,' he said quietly, and even that one word, uttered in his resonant voice, seemed electrifying.

'Hello.' It was a weak sound to which she added, 'I'm not late.'

He might not have heard her as he said, 'I'm going to see Paula Gillis; she's disrupting the household. I shall probably have to send her into a nursing home for psychiatric treatment.'

'A pity,' Emma said, 'we cannot give tablets of courage, instead of tranquillisers. She never studied her husband when he was alive—merely worried him to death.'

Simon threw his medical bag in the back of his car. 'I can't quarrel with that assessment,' he said solemnly. 'Verity wants to go for a run, by the way.' He didn't mention the Gilmores.

And neither did Emma. But she stood and watched his car go down the drive.

It was late that same night, before Emma was asleep, that Verity's bell rang, seeming to send a shudder through the house.

'I'm seeing double,' she cried, almost hysterically, when Simon and Emma joined her, rushing from their respective rooms in anxious apprehension. 'I was reading and——' She gave a frantic cry, 'I had this before, when the M.S. started, but it went away . . .'

'And it will again,' said Simon with more sympathy than conviction, because there was no specific pattern by which to judge the progression of the disease.

She rubbed her eyes. 'Now it's different,' she gasped. 'I can't see your face, Simon, but I can see all round it . . . and if I can't *see* properly——'

Emma took her hand soothingly.

'It will pass,' she said with confidence.

'How do you *know*?'

'Didn't Simon say it would go away? He's the doctor.'

Verity lay back on the pillows, exhausted. Simon gave her a mild sedative and he and Emma stayed with her until she went to sleep. The house was eerie and silent as they tip-toed from the room.

'*Will* she be all right?' Emma asked fearfully, as they reached the hall.

'Pray God so. Symptoms come and go; we don't know what we're up against. I'll get Odile to go over her tomorrow. We *could* do another lumbar puncture, but——' His voice died away wearily and hopelessly.

And all the time Emma was trying not to dwell on the fact that he was wearing the same dressing gown as on that fateful night. In imagination she felt the warmth of his body against hers and, choked with emotion, overwhelmed by longing, said abruptly, knowing she must escape, 'Goodnight . . .

we'll pray for a miracle so that she is better in the morning.' And although Emma was shaking, her voice was controlled.

'Goodnight.' He turned away and walked towards his study without a backward glance.

Once there, he sat down at his desk and bowed his head in his hands, murmuring aloud, 'Oh God, Emma; if you only *knew*!'

CHAPTER SIX

AUTUMN rushed towards winter, during which time Verity reached a state of remission where, apart from her stiff leg, she appeared to be almost normal. Her sight gave no further trouble, her spirits were excellent, and her moods more predictable. Emma continued to minister to her needs, however, while increasing the amount of time spent in the practice.

Odile said suddenly, and unexpectedly, at the end of an evening surgery, 'Emma, may I ask you a personal question?'

While feeling immediately apprehensive, Emma managed to reply casually, 'Of course.'

'Then why are you and Simon so distant to each other these days?' She seemed to hang on Emma's reply.

Emma, guarded, replied, 'We've hardly had time for any cosy chats lately.'

'It isn't that,' Odile persisted. 'You're friendly, but so impersonal.'

Emma watched Odile's expression carefully. Was that anxiety in her eyes?

'You forget I'm part of the household, Odile. One of the family.' She added brightly, 'Or it could be a question of familiarity—we're used to each other.'

Odile exclaimed indiscreetly, 'I shouldn't have thought Simon was the type of man any woman could—could——' She stopped, embarrassed, lowering her gaze and then rushing on, 'I see your point. At one time I thought you were going to have trouble with Verity, but because she's in a remission phase, don't delude yourself that she is any the less possessive where Simon is concerned.' Odile studied Emma intently, 'I suppose Stephen being in the picture helps.'

Was a question concealed in the comment? Emma asked herself. A wave of sympathy surged over her as she looked at Odile. It was an ironical situation. And Emma's mind went back to the first evening she visited Odile's cottage.

Almost as though reading Emma's thoughts, Odile said, 'Thank you for keeping the secret of Simon's visits to me. I knew I could trust you.'

Emma said frankly, 'But Verity knows that Simon sees you at the cottage.'

'Only when it suits him to tell her.' Odile added, 'I often wonder how all this will end. If Verity relapses and then deteriorates . . . Simon will be tied more and more.'

Emma didn't want any drama injected into the situation. 'I suppose so; but let's not be too gloomy. Things have a way of working out, you know.'

Odile sighed. 'I wish I had your optimism. Simon

gets depressed about the future; we often discuss it.'

Emma's heart hurt in that moment. If only Simon would talk to *her*. Even so, any jealousy she might feel was not directed towards Odile as a person, but rather towards a relationship that was full of imponderables. Common sense, however, emphasised that, were Simon in love with Odile, he would marry her—despite Verity. Looking at Odile in that moment, Emma was doubly certain of Odile's love for him, and of her uncertainty where his affections were concerned. Emma held the conviction that Simon, when it came to it, merely loved Simon. He was an impossible man to understand.

'Tomorrow,' Emma began, and stopped, memory stabbing.

Simon overheard the word as he came into Emma's office.

'What about tomorrow?' he asked with a quiet significance.

'Nothing really,' Odile hastened. '*I've* got to think of the next half-hour!' She glanced at the clock. 'I must see Owen about some X-rays, and make one or two telephone calls.' With that she hurried away.

Simon and Emma faced each other almost solemnly. During the past weeks Emma had endeavoured to behave precisely as Odile had described—'friendly but impersonal'. The alternative was to leave Hunter's Close and probably never see Simon again. But no matter what she might suffer through living in close proximity to him, at least he was not wholly lost to her. She hadn't any illusions: obviously Simon was grateful for her attitude, and made no attempt to intrude in her life.

But at that moment emotion crept back. What was he thinking? Feeling? And where had those two lovers of yesterday gone?

He said conversationally, 'I wanted a word with you about Christmas.'

'Christmas,' she echoed, as though it were foreign.

'It is only a month away ... I wondered if you might like to spend it with friends——' He paused for a second and said, 'Or, rather, if you'd care for a holiday?'

Emma winced. Was he *so* anxious to get her out of the house?

'Because Verity is much better?' Emma dropped her voice, 'I don't need to take a *holiday* if you no longer need me here.'

He protested vigorously, 'That doesn't come into it.' He held her gaze with a masterful determination. 'You know perfectly well it doesn't.'

'On the contrary,' she managed to say, wanting to be coldly cynical, while finding that only her love for him had any meaning. 'But I haven't any plans for Christmas. In fact, I haven't thought about it.'

He seemed to put the universe between them as he said in measured tones, 'Then should you wish to spend it away from here, we can manage. My mother would naturally miss you——' He stopped.

'My mother'; not *we*.

Emma struggled to sound calm. 'Thank you, but I doubt if I shall want to go anywhere, unless it is to the Gilmores for an hour or two.' It was as though a game of charades was being skillfully played.

There was a moment of silence before Simon asked, rather like an actor throwing away a line,

'Are you going to marry Stephen?' There was nothing in his manner to betray his reactions to the possibility.

Emma's composure vanished before a sudden wave of emotion, and she said witheringly, 'No; in fact marriage is the last thing I want.' And even as she uttered the words, she realised how easily they could be misconstrued, and added swiftly, 'or any emotional ties.' A knife plunged into her heart, sharpened on regret. That remark made matters even worse, and could be taken as a judgment on the past.

'I see,' said Simon, in a low haunting voice. 'Then any further question would be superfluous.'

She wanted to cry out—to take back the indictment of everything she most desired.

But as though nothing of importance had been said, he picked up a file that was lying on her desk. 'This is Mrs Morris's . . . I came to collect it.'

Emma managed to say, thankful to escape into professionalism, 'I'm sorry she now has thrombophlebitis.'

'Yes; I'm not happy about her. She was very grateful to you for bandaging her leg.'

Emma nodded, never having been nearer to tears, or nearer to getting up and throwing her arms around his neck. Instead, she said, 'I like Mrs Morris and am glad to help her. She will find resting a very wearying process.'

Simon looked down at Emma as she sat there; his gaze searching, uncomprehending. For a second it seemed he was about to say something important, then, his expression changing, he exclaimed, 'Time for you to stop working. With luck we should have a quiet evening.'

After he had gone, Emma sat disconsolately, asking herself why, in moments of emotional strain, one invariably said the wrong thing, or conveyed the wrong impression. But the sense of loss, of insecurity, was like an aching wound; and Simon's quiet acceptance, a whip-lash. If she had any sense, she argued, she would leave Hunter's Close now, while Verity was in a state of remission. Her cheeks reddened as memories swirled back. She had wanted, and given, love; not for a night, but for a lifetime; and she could not now run to other arms. The commitment remained.

Brett called out, 'Goodnight,' and the surgery door shut. Emma dragged herself to her feet, dreading the prospect of the hours ahead. 'With luck we should have a quiet evening', Simon had said. She didn't want a 'quiet evening'. She wanted Yesterday.

Odile went to see Verity before leaving Hunter's Close that evening, and stayed for a drink while Emma was changing. Simon was in his study.

Odile spoke with a trace of excitement, 'I shouldn't be surprised if we have an engagement in the practice before very long.'

'Engagement!' Verity's voice was sharp, and the word came on a breath of apprehension.

'Stephen and Emma.' Odile sipped her gin and tonic. 'I think they'd make a splendid couple, and it would delight us all.'

Relief showed in Verity's beaming smile. 'I *have* wondered . . . so *you* think it is serious?'

'Not on account of anything that has been said,' Odile replied honestly. 'Just a feeling I had when I was talking to Emma this evening.' Odile stopped awkwardly. 'But that wouldn't be too good for you—losing Emma, I mean?'

'I'm so much better,' Verity said, 'that I could almost manage on my own. Oh, I'd miss Emma dreadfully, but her happiness means a great deal to me. Besides, she'd be staying in the district, even if she gave up her job in the practice.'

Odile sighed. 'I don't know what we'd do without her now. She's exactly what we needed, and everyone likes her . . . but we'll meet that trouble when it arises.' Odile gave a little laugh. 'I could be wrong about it all, of course.'

'I hope you're not,' Verity said stoutly.

Odile was left with the feeling that Verity would be delighted by any arrangement, provided Simon was not involved, and her heart sank.

After Odile had gone, and Simon had joined her, Verity repeated the conversation.

'Woman's gossip,' he scoffed.

'Odile doesn't gossip,' Verity protested. 'Neither do I. It would be an ideal marriage.'

Simon's voice was raised slightly, 'Marriage is the last thing Emma wants.'

Verity smiled, a secretive little smile. 'Sometimes you are very naïve.'

Simon poured himself out a larger whisky than usual. He could not very well quote Emma to substantiate his belief.

Emma came into the room at that moment, aware of the undercurrent, but ignoring it as she held out an air-mail letter.

'I've only just read this,' she said, looking from face to face. 'It's from Hugh and Clare. They want us to go to stay with them for Christmas and New Year. There's a special message for you——' She handed Verity the letter as she spoke. In it, Clare had emphasised that there was a ground-floor bedroom and bathroom which would be ideal for Verity, and that she could be guaranteed every comfort.

'Kenya,' Simon said, looking inquiringly at Emma. 'How do you feel about it?'

'Excited,' she admitted, wishing that there were no reservations. 'But with mixed feelings.'

'*You* could go, anyway,' he suggested.

Emma felt utterly forlorn. How readily he favoured the possibility.

Verity spoke up forcefully. 'I'd *love* to go. And Emma would make me feel safe. I'm so much better, but to have a doctor *and* a nurse with me! What more could I ask?'

'There's no reason why you and Emma should not go,' Simon suggested, wondering if Emma's 'mixed feelings' embraced leaving Stephen.

Verity insisted, 'I'd want you to come, Simon. After all, it may be the last opportunity I shall ever have to go away.' There was a pathetic note in her voice. She was well aware that remissions might not last forever. 'Travelling, with a man in charge, is very much simpler . . .. And I'd need a chair to the plane . . . why don't you *say* something?' Her voice rose. 'Or don't you want to go?'

Simon evaded the direct question by exclaiming, 'It's a question of my getting away.'

Emma put in, 'And whether you would agree to my leaving the work——'

'I've already said that you could go,' he interrupted firmly.

'I wasn't regarding myself as indispensable,' Emma flashed back.

'I want us all to go,' Verity insisted in a tone of voice that held finality. 'You can arrange it perfectly well if you want to, Simon.' She was the matriarch giving an order. Then she changed her mood and became cajoling. 'It would be such a wonderful change for me. I haven't been anywhere for so long . . . and to be with Hugh and Clare! Not like some impersonal hotel . . . Oh, Simon, say we can go.'

Emma asked herself if she could endure being with Simon, on holiday; in the tropics, with all that embraced. Tension and suspense built up as she waited for his reply.

'I'll talk to the others about it,' he promised. 'After all, the burden would fall on them.'

'You are always ready to let *them* go off,' Verity said. 'You never get away.'

Simon couldn't remind her that, since her illness, his going had not been feasible—at least not until Emma's advent. He'd had greater peace of mind by remaining at Hunter's Close. At that moment he felt sudden apprehension. There was no guarantee, because Verity was almost back to normal now, that she would continue to be, thus the hazard of her travelling was a consideration. Equally, he had no desire to take a defeatist attitude, which would encourage fears. If she felt she wanted to go, that was half the battle.

'Naturally your parents will want to know as soon as possible,' Simon said, addressing Emma.

'Oh,' Emma assured him airily, 'they wouldn't mind if we arrived out of the blue—any time.'

'But it is Christmas we're discussing,' Simon reminded her. 'People usually plan ahead for that.'

Emma had a little bleak feeling that the last thing he wanted was to go to Kenya with her and Verity.

'We could go to the coast—to Mombasa,' Verity said eagerly. 'And perhaps to one of the game parks.'

'Let's get there first,' Simon suggested dryly.

Verity made an impatient sound.

'You've no *enthusiasm*,' she chided. 'Has he, Emma? Can't you persuade him?'

'I'm the last person,' Emma said.

'It isn't a question of being persuaded,' Simon countered. 'It's a question of——' He stopped abruptly, avoiding Emma's gaze. 'Anyway, as I've already said, I'll discuss it with the others.'

This he did the following evening at the end of a particularly heavy surgery.

It was Odile who spoke first, after Simon had outlined the facts.

'Kenya?' Her voice was startled and fearful. 'For how long?'

Emma sensed the unease with which Odile contemplated the trip.

'Three weeks—a month if possible. What do you think?' He glanced from face to face.

Stephen looked agitated and exclaimed, 'If Emma weren't going——'

Simon cut in, 'There's no question of the

trip without Emma.'

Brett made an expansive gesture, 'You go; we'll cope. There's the Christmas break, anyway, when even the most exacting patients don't grudge us time to tackle the turkey! Splendid opportunity and, by heaven, with three of us here, we should be able to hold the fort.' He gave a goodhumoured grin. 'We shall miss Emma more than you!'

Simon looked at Odile and said tentatively, 'Do you think it fair?'

There was a strained expression on Odile's face; life seemed to have ebbed from her, but she said with an attempt at brightness, 'More than fair. Brett's right. Also, you haven't had a break for far too long . . . we shall survive for a month. Don't worry, you'll have a practice to come back to!'

Stephen murmured flatly, 'Of course.' The thought of a month without Emma appalled him.

'I appreciate it,' Simon said quietly. 'Verity has already set her heart on going, and while she is so much better, I'd hate to deny her the pleasure.'

Odile could not resist saying, 'I can't see your ever denying Verity anything. It should be a wonderful holiday.' She turned to Emma, 'I envy you—in the nicest way.'

'My parents would be only too happy for you to go out for a holiday whenever you could arrange it,' Emma said warmly.

Odile looked grateful, but sad. 'I'd love to go,' she said, 'but not alone.'

'You wouldn't be alone for long,' Simon said significantly.

Odile looked at him for a second and then

averted her gaze.

Emma watched in silence, her thoughts flying back to a conversation held when she first arrived at Hunter's Close and Simon had, in discussing Kenya, spoken of 'the three of us' going on holiday there. And she had wondered, even then, how far Verity dominated his life. Yet to suggest that he was a man easily led, or influenced, seemed blatantly absurd. Verity's hold came into a different category; her complaint a weapon in itself.

An uncomfortable silence fell; the atmosphere charged with the unruly thoughts of each one, making them awkward and ill at ease.

Stephen said stiffly, 'How soon do you intend to go?'

'Early enough for Verity to get settled in for Christmas. The journey shouldn't present any problems.'

'Provided Verity remains in her present state,' Stephen warned, jealousy goading him.

'There are hazards in everything. I can't remind her of them at every turn,' Simon said resolutely.

Stephen sighed, half-apologetically.

'Of course not,' he murmured.

The little gathering broke up. Emma felt the weight of Stephen's depression, to which was added Odile's sadness. Only Brett looked confident and carefree.

Simon and Emma were left alone in a little dark pool of uncertainty.

'Hardly whole-hearted support,' he commented, his gaze falling on her with a provocative inquiry.

'Nor any opposition,' she said.

'Stephen will miss you,' Simon suggested darkly.

'Hearts don't break in a month,' she retorted.

Simon's lips parted and then closed into a hard line.

They moved to the door and when they reached it his shoulder pressed against hers, and it was as though a flame seared her. Their awareness was immediate; and her rejection swift, as she moved to escape further contact.

'I'll ring my parents,' she said quickly, trying to remain calm.

'A good idea. It's very kind of them to invite us.' His voice was polite and formal. 'At least this will be one way of your seeing them.' He opened the door as he spoke.

'I don't think you will be too bored,' Emma said pointedly. 'The knowledge that you are giving Verity pleasure will make up for any defects.'

He looked down at her with pained speculation. 'And is that the yardstick by which you measure my enjoyment?'

'Mostly,' she admitted. 'In the circumstances one can hardly fault it.' And even as she spoke she knew that she had now become a past master at cynical observations, words tumbling out of her brain with hopeless lack of co-ordination.

'Don't sugar-coat the pill, Emma,' he warned.

She shrivelled emotionally, longing to reach out to him, to tell him that love was an agony and that attack was the only weapon with which she could combat her own vulnerability. She dare not weaken, because she would betray herself and be at his mercy.

'*You* write out the prescriptions, don't forget.' She flashed him a scathing look and went ahead down the covered way to the house.

Dinner was nearly over that evening when an agitated Jessop appeared, saying, 'A patient, Doctor, in a—a—bad way——' Jessop's usual composure deserted him.

In that second a sharp cry came from the hall, and both Simon and Emma hurried out.

A young girl, flaxen-haired, in her early twenties—fur coat over a nightdress—was slumped on the floor.

'The baby—it's coming,' she gasped. 'I'm Wendy . . . Wendy Farrar—Mrs——'

Emma acted quickly, running to the surgery and returning with a wheel-chair in which they managed to get the patient to Simon's consulting room, and on to the examining couch.

'So . . . *sorry*,' the words came between great agonising breaths.

On examination, Simon found it to be a case of precipitate labour, all stages following one another very quickly.

'No time to get you to hospital,' he said, and turning swiftly to Emma, added, 'full dilation——'

Emma was already marshalling necessities; receptacles, hot water, sterile pads and towels from an emergency cupboard. She had hardly finished when the child, a boy, thrust itself into the world with aggressive speed, his lusty cry subsequently piercing the quiet of Hunter's Close like a siren. After a short while, the placenta expelled, he was placed (towel-wrapped) in his mother's arms, as she lay propped up on pillows which Emma had grabbed from the household linen cupboard.

Simon, beaming, thankful to have been spared complications, exclaimed, 'The first time my consulting room has been used as a labour ward! You left it a bit late, Mrs Farrar!'

'I wasn't given much time, either . . . he wasn't due for another fortnight, and I'm booked into a London nursing home. We live there, and come down here, to White Cottage, when we can. My husband had to go up to London on business today, and was due back any moment. When the pain increased, and the contractions became more frequent, I panicked, got in my car and rushed here. It's only about a quarter of a mile.' She gave a little nervous laugh. 'I knew of you . . . and that you were near . . . I'm so sorry to have caused all this upheaval.'

'Pleasure,' Simon assured her, 'provided you don't make a habit of it! You've got a fine son, anyway. Now I'll send for an ambulance and get you into the nursing home.'

There was an immediate protest.

Simon was firm. 'You will not go back to London for a few days. I'm quite sure your husband will agree with me.' Simon added a trifle anxiously, 'Does he know where you are?'

'Yes; I scribbled your name and address . . . he should be here at any moment. Oh, dear! I really *am* so sorry to have given you all this trouble.'

Simon flashed Emma a little significant smile.

'We've enjoyed it, haven't we, Nurse?'

Emma felt the warmth of his response, and prized that moment of closeness.

'Are you really a nurse?'

'Really.'

'And now,' Simon said, 'I'll leave you in Nurse's care.'

When he had gone, Wendy Farrar gave a little laugh.

'I certainly chose a very charming doctor! But what an introduction! And I was too scared to be embarrassed . . . Adrian—my husband—and I, have been at the cottage for ten days—our last visit this year, most probably. My mother is looking after our daughter, Lucinda, so that we could have the break.'

'How old is Lucinda?'

'Two and a half.' A little sigh of pleasure followed the reply.

'You must rest,' Emma admonished.

'I feel fine.' Twinkling eyes met Emma's. 'You've been marvellous. I don't know what I should have *done*! Even if I'd rung for an ambulance I'd have given birth before it arrived! I didn't really explain to Dr Conway, but we were going to contact him in case of any emergencies down here.' She looked across to the chair where the newly-born child was now sleeping, wrapped like a mummy. 'I can't believe he's here—or that I've had him so easily! We're going to call him Jonathan . . . what is Dr Conway's name?'

'Simon.' Even uttering the name filled Emma with emotion.

'Then we shall make it Jonathan Simon . . . would he mind?'

'He'd be honoured, I imagine.'

There was a momentary silence before Wendy Farrar exclaimed, 'Thank goodness I came in a nightdress! I'd just had my bath, intending to go to bed and rest before Adrian returned ... oh, heavens!' she rushed on, 'I haven't any baby clothes down here. Adrian will have to buy some tomorrow. I do hope he won't be too shocked and upset by my note ... what is the time?'

'Nine o'clock ... I've nearly finished with you.'

'If only Adrian could come before the ambulance arrives. I don't want to go anywhere except home, but there's no one to look after us at the cottage, and Adrian couldn't cope alone, although he's wonderful.'

'It won't be very long before you can be driven back to London.'

'No, of course.' It was a delighted happy sound.

Hearing it made Emma shrink from her own heartache. For a short while the patient and the baby had absorbed time and thought. Now, gradually, the bleak sensation was returning. Here was a young girl so obviously happy that its bloom lay upon her. Married; with two children. *'Don't sugar-coat the pill, Emma.'* And she knew that all harmony seemed to have disappeared from her relationship with Simon.

'Would you hear the front door bell?' Wendy Farrar's cheeks flushed. 'I wish Adrian would come ... I thought I heard a bell.'

Emma finished her ministrations and smoothed the house-coat she had loaned the mother. 'Now you are ready to receive him—you look lovely.'

'Bless you.' A hand touched Emma's in gratitude.

'You've made it all so easy and natural.'

Adrian Farrar arrived at that moment, looking like a man on the verge of a heart attack.

'Don't worry,' Simon said reassuringly, 'your wife's fine. No problems . . . I'll find out if you can see her——'

'But——'

'Just give me one minute.' Simon hurried away, spoke to Emma to make sure her work was done, and then led the dazed, anxious husband to the consulting room, urging him through the door saying, 'Your wife will want to tell you all about it!'

Emma moved to Simon's side and they stood in a little oasis of professional satisfaction as their eyes met. 'Someone,' he murmured, 'I forget who, wrote "how bitter a thing it is to see happiness through another's eyes". Unlike you, I envy those two. They, obviously, have a real marriage. We get few, heaven knows, in our job.'

There was a long tense pause, then Simon added, 'You were splendid. I don't know how on earth I'd have coped without you.'

A sob rose in Emma's throat, choking her. She stood mute, tormented. And *she* had said that the very last thing she wanted was marriage. Could she now complain if Simon took her at her word? And what could she deduce from his remarks? If he envied the Farrars, why didn't he emulate them?

A little while later they watched the ambulance drive away with a radiant, if tired, mother, a chubby healthy baby, and an excited, concerned, and bewildered husband.

The subject of Kenya came up again that evening,

just before Emma was about to go to bed. Verity was already settled, and the house had the silence of approaching night.

'I want to be quite sure about this proposed holiday,' Simon said solemnly.

'Sure? In what way?' She felt uneasy.

'The fact that your parents have invited Verity and me does not automatically mean you are enthusiastic about the trip. "Mixed feelings" hardly suggest delight.' His voice hardened slightly. 'Much as I would hate to disappoint my mother, I would prefer it to finding myself in a situation where your hostility marred everything.'

'*My* hostility,' she gasped, seething.

'Perhaps it is too harsh a word,' he corrected, 'but I think you know what I mean.'

'I hardly think you can fault my behaviour to Verity, and if we go to Kenya I shall do everything possible to see that she enjoys herself to the full.'

'I'm not seeking concessions,' he retorted, voice raised.

'And I wasn't making them,' she blazed.

The sound of anger vibrated between them like wrong notes crashing from a piano. All the pent up fury, frustration and desire, swirled them into the danger zone of truth. Memories lay between them like raw wounds for which there was no palliative. He turned away, breathing deeply, afraid of losing control.

After an electric silence, emotion spent, he said quietly, 'Then suppose we end this acrimony?'

The change of attitude defeated her; strength drained in sudden surrender. She nodded, rather than utter words which might rekindle the flame of their animosity.

'If we left here on about the 15th December . . .' The suggestion was made with calm assessment; he looked at her for confirmation, his expression impassive.

'Whatever you think.' She wasn't avoiding responsibility so much as recognising his greater involvement. He had practice decisions to make. She added, 'You have a lot to take into account.'

'That's true. The Jessops will look after the house, and Odile will be there should they need advice of any kind.'

A breath of sadness touched Emma for Odile's sake. She did not underestimate how greatly Odile would miss Simon during that month. In a strange, wholly irrational, way, Odile's love for him was a bond, not a scourge.

Emma telephoned her parents the following morning, her mood changing as she realised that in a short while, she would be seeing her father and mother, and spending Christmas with them. Hope filtered through from the darkness of anger. Since Simon would be with her, why shouldn't the holiday herald a new beginning? There would be time to talk without the continual demands of patients, and with Verity better, times, also, when she, Emma, and Simon might enjoy exploring parts of Kenya on their own. Gloom vanished in that magical moment when her spirits suddenly soared and, in imagination, a new vista opened up before her. She glanced across the room to where Simon was standing surveying her, as she sat down beside the telephone and lifted the receiver. In the look they exchanged there was a truce that brought a sparkle to her eyes, and a lilt to her voice when her father answered her call.

CHAPTER SEVEN

THERE was heightened activity during the days prior to the arranged flight to Nairobi on December 15th. Simon might have been going away for four years instead of weeks, if the behaviour of his patients was anything to go by, for they bombarded him with requests for prescriptions and last minute visits, each determined not to transfer his, or her, loyalty to the other partners during his absence, unless it became a matter of great urgency.

'All I want,' Simon said to Odile, 'is to get on that plane! Until then——' he made a grimace.

'You're looking forward to it.' The statement concealed sadness at his going.

'Yes; yes, I am,' he admitted, flashing her an inquiring look. 'Do you find that surprising?'

'No,' she said, adding, 'not in the circumstances.' She broke off abruptly and half-apologetically. 'It will seem very strange without you here.'

He looked at her, faintly questioning, and then gave a little unexpected laugh. 'I shall feel strange myself. I'm not in training for holidays!'

'Which isn't surprising, seeing that you never have any . . . at least not since your mother's illness. I hope she is able to stand up to it all.'

'So do I,' he said devoutly.

'Will you go to Mombasa?'

'Who can say? We shall have to play it by ear.'

Odile tried to speak lightly, 'I'm sure Emma's parents will baby-sit so that you and Emma can get away. Hardly worth going otherwise.' She stared him out and he dropped his gaze.

'I'm aware of the hazards, Odile,' he said quietly, 'and of the possibilities.'

She winced, but forced a smile. It was the last conversation she had alone with him before he left.

Meanwhile Emma bought the many things that Verity required—few of the items really essential.

'You don't seem to realise,' Emma pointed out gently, 'that you will be able to buy anything and everything you want in Nairobi. It is a large modern city——'

'I always did like to take things *with* me,' Verity insisted.

'But there is a question of excess baggage,' Emma reasoned.

Verity approached Simon.

'Take what you want,' he said easily. 'We don't go away every day.' He glanced at Emma. 'Don't worry,' he added. 'It won't cost a fortune.'

Verity beamed. 'I knew Simon would understand.' She sighed happily. 'But I know you meant well, Emma, and wanted to save us money.'

'I was really thinking that the lighter one travels, the simpler it becomes.'

'I've never believed in that,' Verity said complacently.

Simon smiled. Emma felt irritated, and then

criticised herself. A little extra packing and shopping wouldn't hurt her, after all.

Nevertheless she was thankful when the 15th arrived and the hall was stacked with baggage. Their flight was at twenty-one hours, which meant checking in at twenty hours.

'I hope the hire car won't be late,' Verity said agitatedly. 'I don't know why you couldn't have let Jessop drive us to Heathrow.'

Simon didn't argue. Jessop was not familiar with Heathrow traffic.

'Do you know the driver?' Verity persisted.

'The owner of the hire firm is a patient of mine,' Simon explained patiently.

'Oh.'

Emma touched Verity's hand reassuringly.

'Just think about being in Kenya tomorrow.'

Stephen came into the drawing room at that moment.

'To wish you all a Happy Christmas,' he said self-consciously, hoping to have had a last word with Emma on her own. He looked at her intently, 'Send me a postcard!' And while he endeavoured to sound cheerful, his depression was obvious.

'We'll take good care of her,' Verity promised, deliberately identifying Emma with him, much to Emma's annoyance.

Simon's mouth hardened.

Jessop appeared, relieving the tension.

'The car is here, Doctor.'

It was one of those cold black nights when the rain came down like rods, and lights left deceptive pools of amber to create shadows that appeared as ghosts, startling and dangerous. Now and again sleet changed the pattern, and the roads, already glass-like, became even more slippery and treacherous. The countryside was obliterated, so that it was like travelling in a dark tunnel where headlights were inadequate against the misty gloom.

'I hate this,' Verity cried out in alarm.

'The wind-screen wipers are the worst irritant,' Simon said.

'Where are we?' Verity peered out anxiously.

'Just approaching Woodstock; we shall soon be on the M40 . . .. You're very quiet, Emma.'

The sound of her name on his lips brought Emma out of her momentary reverie.

'I think silence in a car can be a blessing on occasions,' she said with a little laugh, hastening, in case the remark might appear to be directed against Verity who had been particularly talkative, 'it is only just beginning to register that I shall soon be seeing my parents.'

Simon turned and flashed her an understanding smile. No word was spoken, but Emma's heart seemed to lift as though it had suddenly found a resting place.

Heathrow eventually rose out of the blackness in a blaze of saffron lights, its garishness softened. Emma was only conscious that she was there with Simon. Not in his consulting room; not in a drawing room, but in that strange exciting land of adventure which opened up mysteriously at the beginning of a journey, as though traced on an imaginary map.

And so to Terminal Three, Verity safely in her chair (with a disabled person's attendant to take her into the special reservation and ultimately to see her on the plane, one passenger only allowed to accompany her—in this case, Simon). Noise, clatter, trolleys, baggage thrust into weighing machines, boarding cards collected. People hurrying; people standing waiting, some nonchalantly, some bewildered; others fearful. All races, each in an individual world, eyes turned to a distant horizon. The voice of the announcers echoing hollowly into the vastness, as if from outer space. A commonplace scene, yet, despite its familiarity, always a unique one, because every passenger had a story to tell.

'Now, I'm beginning to believe it's true,' Simon murmured.

Passports; handbags and hand luggage checked and X-rayed. On, on, Simon ahead with Verity, until that moment of relaxing in an allotted seat. Movement, shuffling, passengers getting comfortable; laughter; strained faces, and smiling ones. The air hostess welcoming, the confusion part of their scene and a time for their assessment. Seat belts fastened and, at last, the great throbbing of the engines as they taxied down the runway, turning, shuddering and pulsating, like some wild animal held in check, before that moment of release when the giant aircraft raced faster, faster, until the ground was lost and they were airborne.

'I've only flown once before—just to Paris,' Emma admitted. 'I didn't mention it,' she added, turning in her seat, beside Verity, to look at Simon who was sitting immediately behind her. 'I didn't know if you might think me a liability, or too inexperienced. I'd fly around the world if I could!'

'We'll drink to that,' Simon suggested, and ordered champagne. 'It's an eight-hour flight, so we've plenty of time to enjoy ourselves before we settle down to sleep.'

The word 'sleep' was charged with emotion, as Emma remembered how she and Simon had slept in each other's arms. Almost as though reading her thoughts, he added softly, 'So this will be the first occasion you've slept on a plane?'

'There is a first time for everything,' she replied, turning back in her seat.

Verity was peering out into the inky darkness, complaining that there was nothing to see.

'How far is it to Nairobi?' she asked.

'Four thousand two hundred and thirty-five miles,' Emma answered with alacrity. 'I looked it up,' she added, 'when Hugh and Clare first went there. It's good that you are friends. I sometimes forget the fact.' Emma realised how remote certain aspects of her life had become since she recognised her love for Simon. His nearness at that moment was sweet torture. And when at last the lights of the aircraft dimmed for the night, and they lowered their seats to a reclining position, she lay very still, trying to think of the journey and that they were cutting through the sky, the sound of the engines becoming part of the silence. No one stirred; intermittently, air hostesses walked noiselessly up and down the corridors to make sure that no one needed attention. Was Simon asleep? She could not see, and dare not move, in case she disturbed Verity. And at last, exhausted more by emotion than weariness, she fell asleep.

It was an uneventful flight until they began the

descent into Nairobi. Then, a panorama of white, gold and blue surrounded them; the sun shimmering, the warmth caressing them after the chill damp of the previous night. Red earth and vivid greens spread out like vast paintings tilted against the sky, the views illimitable as the tarmac came nearer and they felt that final sensation of wheels gripping the runway and the powerful braking. In that moment the heat struck them as though an oven door had been opened.

Once out of the plane, it was exactly like a hot English summer day, but without the humidity, for Nairobi was five thousand feet above sea level.

'You may feel a little breathless on exertion,' Simon warned, 'just at first. The altitude has that effect.'

Verity pointed to the waiting-terrace of the spacious white building ahead—Jomo Kenyatta Airport.

Emma was hardly conscious of getting through Customs, or collecting their luggage and being able to see her parents through the glass windows leading to the outer hall. It all had a dreamlike quality about it, which Simon's presence heightened. She felt overwhelmingly shy when the time came to meet her mother's gaze.

'It's just not true,' she gasped, 'being here like this.'

Greetings followed. Verity held court from her chair, looking amazingly fresh after the journey.

Emma was conscious of Simon kissing Clare, and of Hugh gripping Simon's hand as though Simon were a long lost son. And even as she watched, the thought flashed through her mind: 'I have slept with Simon; he was my lover for one night. I know his body, and he mine.' The fact added a new dimension to the situation. Would her mother suspect her love for Simon? And find answers to the questions she would never ask? Emma squared her shoulders, breathed deeply, and mechanically took her place in Clare's car. Hugh ushered Verity and Simon into his, because it was larger and more comfortable for Verity.

'You look fantastic, Clare,' Emma exclaimed, using the Christian name, as was mostly her custom. 'Your tan! It makes your eyes so blue—and your hair's much lighter.'

'Bleached by the sun.'

They drove from the airport—situated on the Athi River plains—and headed for Karen.

'We skirt Nairobi,' Clare explained, 'and are only about twelve miles from our house.'

'The weather's so heavenly.'

The vastness of scrub and plain was difficult to absorb after the miniature landscape of England. Massive banks of white cloud billowed as though they were decorations hung from a vast backcloth of deepest blue.

'We can organise a picnic on any day, or week, and know it will be fine,' Clare said with a little laugh. 'The weather isn't a topic of conversation!'

'A picnic.' Emma despised herself. Here she was in Africa for the first time, and at the mention of the word, 'picnic', all she could think about was an autumn evening with Simon! She managed to say, 'How lovely', and in that moment felt years older than her mother, who was forty-eight and looked years younger; her hair loose and natural; her skin untouched by make-up, except for lipstick, because her tan was adornment in itself.

'That's the Nairobi National Park on your left,' Clare pointed out, and a little later explained, indicating the rolling countryside, 'Just here we can sometimes see Mount Kenya on the one side and Kilimanjaro on the other.'

When they reached Karen, Emma said, 'It reminds me of an English residential area somewhere on the Surrey-Hampshire borders—apart from the red soil and the grass—it's almost emerald green.' There was wonderment in her voice as she spoke.

'Kikuyu grass,' Clare told her.

'It's magnificent set against that unbelievably blue sky.' Emma knew she was resorting to 'tourist' comments, rather than introduce a more personal note.

But Clare said, 'And all's well at Hunter's Close? I mean, you like working there?'

'Very much. I've learnt a great deal.'

'And Simon?'

'He's a very fine doctor.'

Clare gave a little chuckle. 'And is a very attractive man. Don't tell me you haven't noticed!' She shot Emma a sideways glance, aware that Emma's expression was wary. 'Here we are,' she added, to Emma's relief, as they turned into a short drive leading to Mitha Lodge, a flat-roofed, white house, with three balconies shaded by red-and-white striped awnings, to soften the glare of the sun in the bedrooms. The front door was placed centrally, with a deep porch over which a petrea climbed, its large racemes of violet-blue flowers filling the air with fragrance. Mitha Lodge stood in five acres and was surrounded by indigenous trees and blossoming shrubs.

Once out of the car Emma paused, entranced, turning eagerly as Hugh's car came up the drive. She wanted to share these first impressions with Simon, and while Hugh and Clare were seeing Verity into the house, Emma moved so that she and Simon stood together, taking in the beauty of the scene.

'I feel I'm suddenly in many countries at once,' she murmured, 'and shall never forget the deep blue of the sky—the vastness, or the—the——' She stopped.

'The—what?' he prompted gently, looking down at her and waiting.

She wanted to say, 'the fact that we both saw Kenya for the first time *together*,' but added swiftly, 'the strange sensation of knowing one is in the tropics, while standing in what might almost be an English garden—carnations, hibiscus, lilies, roses all blooming at once! And this perfect weather in December!'

'You look bewitched,' he said.

A lizard darted across a rockery nearby, very close to Emma's feet. She gave a little cry and instinctively put a hand on Simon's arm.

He laughed, but his fingers closed on hers and remained there for a fraction of a second, emotion like a pulse throbbing between them.

'We must go in,' she said swiftly.

Her father's tall figure appeared in the square hall as they entered it. Hugh Reade was an uncomplicated man, easy-going, brilliant at his job, and contented with his life. If his temperament did not take him to any great heights, neither did it plunge him

into any depths, and his good temper was a buffer
against Clare's more volatile nature. They comple-
mented each other. And if the moonlit African nights
aroused Clare to greater passion than Hugh could
attain, no complaint was made. The credits were
weighed against the debits and the marriage was
eminently satisfactory. Emma had always known a
'happy home', and the description in general
papered over a multitude of cracks.

'Let me have a look at you,' Hugh said, putting a
hand on her shoulder. Emma was closer to her father
than to her mother, in that unspoken fashion which
deepened the bond. He glanced at Simon. 'We're so
delighted that she's with you and Verity,' he added.

There was a second's pause before Simon said,
'We're delighted, too.' Simon looked about him,
feeling suddenly isolated.

Mitha Lodge was a spacious house, with large
rooms and windows and every modern comfort. A
red brick Dutch-type fireplace took up almost one
wall of the drawing room and bore testimony to the
fact that, in Kenya, when darkness fell at about seven
in the evening, it was sometimes cool enough for a
fire to add comfort, even though it might not be a
necessity. Cedarwood logs were burned and the smell
was part of the magic of the nights. The floors
throughout the house were of highly-polished wood,
in which antique furniture was mirrored, blending
with the sunlight. Flowers of every hue and description decorated each room, and a grandfather clock
ticked away into the silence as though it held all the
secrets of life and time.

'A bath,' Emma said swiftly.

'We can do a nice line in bathrooms in this house,' Hugh said with a grin. 'Verity has hers; we have ours, and there's a "spare" which you and Simon can fight over! Your rooms are next to it! But there's a shower in the downstairs cloak-room. The lady from whom we took the house was disabled, and had it put in specially.' He made an expansive gesture, 'So take your choice.'

'The bath's mine,' Emma said, looking at Simon and suddenly realising that, in her parents' home, she had a freedom lacking at Hunter's Close, no matter how welcome she had been made there. And with freedom came confidence, and a determination to make the most of this holiday, and live one day at a time. She stopped, suddenly remembering Verity almost as though she had, until then, ceased to exist.

'I must go and see if Verity needs me,' she said swiftly, looking about her, lost.

'Through the glass door on your left, down the corridor and turn right,' Hugh directed.

Verity and Clare were talking, Verity lying on the bed. Now she looked tired, and Emma's heart sank. The uncertainty of her condition created permanent suspense.

'I won't bath yet,' she announced, smiling at Emma. 'But I need my small case unpacked.'

Clare glanced from face to face, half-questioning. It sank in that Emma was looking after Verity, as well as helping Simon.

'I've the best nurse in the world,' Verity said.

Outside the bedroom some minutes later, when Verity was settled and wishing to sleep, Clare said, 'Is she very exacting, Emma?'

'All patients are naturally a little self-centred,' Emma replied.

'I'll do all I can while you're here,' came the swift promise. 'I want you to enjoy yourself. And have some freedom . . . Verity has already spoken of us all going to Mombasa. Far better if you and Simon were to go off on your own.'

'Simon might not agree with you,' Emma said unguardedly. 'This is very much Verity's holiday.'

'But——' Clare was not unmindful of Verity's natural determination to have her own way, and already felt defensive in Emma's cause.

'We'll let things take their course, Clare,' Emma said with emphasis.

'How bad is her leg?'

'Stiff; but it varies. She cannot get into the bath, or out of it, without help . . . didn't you realise?'

'In a vague way, I suppose. She seems different somehow.'

'An ever-changing pattern. People get accustomed to being looked after and the centre of attention, don't forget.' Emma laughed. 'And don't start worrying!'

Clare looked troubled. Until that moment it hadn't registered that Emma was, after all, tied to her patient to a certain extent.

'I thought "remission" meant being able to live a normal life,' Clare persisted.

'It does, up to a point,' Emma explained. 'Symptoms come and go without warning, or apparent reason. And there are personality changes.' Emma paused and then added hastily, 'One adjusts to varying moods. So don't be alarmed if you find her a little temperamental on occasion.'

'It must be quite an ordeal for Simon.' Clare felt slightly guilty because it had been easy to accept the fact that Verity's condition had improved, and to lose sight of the overall gravity.

Emma was grateful that Simon came towards them at that moment, so she was spared comment. He had an expression of inquiry on his face.

'Verity's having a rest,' Emma told him.

Clare watched Simon carefully, aware of his concern.

'Oh, good. She stood the journey well . . . now I can have a shower.'

'And breakfast immediately afterwards,' Clare suggested. 'I'm sure you didn't eat much on the plane.'

'Breakfast!' Emma made an approving sound.

'About half-an-hour's time? On the veranda.' Clare added, 'We live out there until evening.'

Half-an-hour later they all gathered at the long, beautifully arranged table, with its dazzlingly white napery and attractive china. Luscious tropical fruits followed by eggs, bacon, sausages and freshly-made coffee, stimulated their appetite and created a feeling of leisured luxury. The grounds spread out before them, the emerald shaded grass and flower-filled smaller gardens, blazing their colour against the brilliant blue sunlit sky.

'What is that heavenly smell?' Emma asked, turning her head towards a flowering plant massed near the drive.

'Frangipani.'

'It looks like a pink star, and smells a little like syringa——' Emma shook her head in disbelief. 'It is difficult to believe all this is real! The scent—I mean, one doesn't expect it in the tropics, somehow.'

'Altitude,' Hugh said. 'Everything grows and retains its fragrance here, in this red earth. And before the rains, you can have parts of the country as brown as a donkey's back, and after three days all will be as green as you see it now.'

Emma said injudiciously, 'I wish they could see it at Hunter's Close.'

Simon didn't wait a second before he exclaimed, 'Yes, Stephen would like all this.'

Emma's voice was cold, 'I wasn't thinking only of Stephen . . . *Verity*———!'

Verity was walking slowly towards them, rather drawn and faintly reproachful. 'I called,' she said, a little plaintively. 'And lost my way . . . so many twists and turns here, Clare! . . . Emma, would you turn on my bath?' Simon and Hugh got to their feet. Simon looked around and, seeing a comfortable chair, urged Verity towards it. She sat down, stick beside her, and glancing at the table said, 'Breakfast! I'd like to have joined you.'

'But you wanted to rest,' Clare put in gently.

'Have you all finished?'

There was an almost guilty silence before Clare hastened, 'We can get you anything you like.'

'Just coffee . . . I hate eating alone . . . it's very warm, isn't it?' There was a note of complaint in her voice.

'Gloriously warm,' Emma cried, stroking her bare arms and looking at her primrose yellow cotton dress. 'After that car journey last night———' She saw the resistant expression on Verity's face. 'Do you want your bath immediately?'

'No; I'll sit and have my coffee first.'

Clare flashed Hugh an uneasy glance. Was this to be the pattern of the holiday?

Emma noticed at that moment how handsome Simon looked in his light grey trousers, and open-necked white shirt. There was a virility about him that set her heart racing and memory swirling back. As though aware of her gaze upon him, he looked straight into her eyes, catching her completely off guard.

And suddenly, almost sharply, Verity called, 'Emma!'

The spell broke as Emma realised Verity had intercepted that revealing gaze.

'Your bath,' Emma murmured, and got to her feet. Hugh and Clare made a pretext for leaving the table, and followed Emma as she left the veranda.

Simon didn't make any attempt to conceal his annoyance and said, as he looked at Verity, 'Just one thing, Mother: don't forget that Emma is on holiday and that we are Hugh's and Clare's guests. Your manner just now was perfunctory and dictatorial.'

Verity completely ignored his words as she said firmly, 'I want a bell in my room. Perhaps this holiday was not such a good idea after all.'

'What do you mean? We've only just arrived.'

'Emma wouldn't have left Stephen and come with us, had her parents not lived here.' Verity made the suggestion irrelevantly, watching Simon intently as she spoke.

'We're not talking about Stephen,' Simon retorted, his voice slightly raised. 'I want this holiday to be a success and——'

'Are you suggesting that I shall spoil it?' The words were deliberate and uttered in unmistakable staccato fashion.

Hearing the challenge, and realising how symptomatic the intonation was of her disease, Simon relented, and hastened, 'You know I'm not suggesting anything of the kind.' He added, 'This trip wouldn't have been considered, but for you.' Misgiving touched him as he spoke. Had he made a big mistake in believing that Verity would adapt to an entirely unfamiliar environment?

It was not until the afternoon, when Verity was resting, that Hugh and Clare took Simon and Emma on what they termed, 'A Cook's tour of the estate'!

Karen itself lay at the foot of the Ngong Hills, named after the Danish authoress Countess Karen von Blixen—whose house was open to the public—their eight-thousand-foot humps a local landmark.

'The view from the hills,' Hugh said, 'on a clear day, is magnificent and you can see a hundred miles or more across the Rift Valley. Zebra, giraffe, eland and buffalo wander about their slopes ... we were lucky to get this place, furnished, while the owners were away on an extended tour.'

Banana groves covered about half an acre, fruit massed on the trees and almost concealed by their strong stems. Sunlight filtered through them, forming deep cool aisles. Suddenly, overwhelmingly, Emma felt the silent mysterious influence of the tropics, and the first real awareness of a new land. Avocado trees, heavy with their large dark pears (falling like apples at harvest time) stood out sharply, some trees a great height; others smaller. Emma picked up a pear.

'Rattle it,' Clare said.

The stone inside sounded like a ripe almond nut.

'Rather different,' Clare suggested, 'from the mean little samples sometimes served in fashionable London restaurants!'

'And those peppers growing near the ground . . . and mangoes.'

'And guavas,' Clare added, smiling.

Simon pointed to the cauliflowers, beans, peas.

'You'd find it difficult to ask for any fruit or vegetable that doesn't grow here,' Hugh exclaimed, 'but the apples and blackberries are *shensi*!'

'What does that mean?' Emma laughed.

'A Swahili word for poor, indifferent, not up to standard!'

It was while they were having their drinks that evening that Clare said startlingly, and with quiet determination, 'I know you've only been here a very short while——' she looked first at Simon and then Emma, addressing them both, 'but Hugh and I wondered if you would like to spend a few days at the coast before Christmas. Time goes so *quickly*——' She hurried on, 'We'd love to look after Verity and have her to ourselves.' She flashed Verity an endearing smile, 'I promise we'll take the greatest care of her . . . what do you think?'

Emma's heart felt that it was hanging on a breaking thread as she waited for Simon's reply.

Verity's voice crashed into the momentary silence. 'But I——'

Simon might not have heard her; his answer was firm and decisive. 'A splendid idea. There's nothing I'd like more. That is, if Emma is agreeable.'

CHAPTER EIGHT

EMMA heard those words, 'If Emma is agreeable', as though they were music echoing in moonlight. There was no mistaking Simon's enthusiasm for the proposed holiday, and she said eagerly, 'I'd love to go.'

Verity spoke up a trifle sharply, '*I'd* hoped to go to Mombasa. Couldn't we *all* go?'

Clare was gentle, but emphatic. 'I think you'd find it very trying since, already, you consider it hot *here*. Also, it's a five to six hour journey by road, and while, of course, one can fly——' she broke off and then continued, 'I know of old that you don't care very much for the beach, or lying in the sun and, at Mombasa, it would certainly be an outdoor holiday.'

Verity sighed. 'I suppose I must reconcile myself to the fact that even being so much better doesn't allow me to enjoy myself like other people.'

'But you'll be able to enjoy yourself so much here, in Nairobi,' Clare said persuasively, determined that Simon and Emma should have some freedom. 'We'll take you to all the interesting places, and we've friends you'll enjoy meeting.'

Thus it was settled on a note of practicality, without Simon being drawn into any argument.

Dinner that night was an occasion. Twilight had come and gone in half-an-hour and it was cooling after the heat of the day. Candles adorned the table and the serving was done by Ricky, smart in his black trousers and white jacket, and wearing white plimsolls—an expert, who moved noiselessly, his pleasant African face gleaming like polished mahogany. There was a staff of three, and for general housework each wore long trousers, plus bush shirt in khaki.

Every now and then Simon's gaze met Emma's in the flickering, magical light, and when the meal was over and coffee drunk, he said, 'Would you like a walk?'

Emma got a light cream shawl and put it about her shoulders. They walked through to the veranda, down the steps, and into the soft purple-blue night. The star-studded darkness held mystery and enchantment; the moon, like a vast golden lamp, hung low, as though suspended from sapphire velvet. The fragrance of flowers, refreshed after the sun's heat, stood out stereoscopically, the unfamiliar sound of crickets, part of the silence. There was a sensuousness in the atmosphere as the near-warmth caressed them.

'Mombasa,' he said resolutely, 'is a splendid idea.'

'Yes.' She was tense, even apprehensive. Was she mad to have agreed to go with him—alone?

He turned and looked down at her, his eyes dark, desirous.

She lowered her gaze, fearing he might see the love she was struggling to hide.

And suddenly, almost roughly, he drew her towards him, his lips parting hers, sinking into the moist warmth of her mouth in inescapable passion.

For a second she surrendered and then, with determination, drew back. She wanted words; she wanted tangible proof of love, not merely sexual need, physical expression, but permanence and commitment. So, she had told him that she didn't want any involvement, but it was up to him to challenge that!

Simon let her go and made no attempt to kiss her again. The incident might not have happened as he said, after a short while, 'We'd better go in.'

Verity eyed them with curiosity born of faint suspicion, as they returned to the drawing room. Emma's cheeks were flushed, an air of confusion hung about her.

'A brandy,' Hugh suggested.

'Please,' Emma said in a breath, avoiding her father's slightly inquiring gaze.

'It struck me,' Hugh said, addressing Simon, 'that I could book you in at the Nyali Beach Hotel. We know the place and——'

'Fine,' Simon agreed, making a gesture that embraced Emma.

Emma managed to look at Simon. 'We could go on the 18th,' she suggested, her manner casual, 'have a long week-end and be back before Christmas Eve.'

It was settled. Hugh telephoned and arranged the rooms.

The following morning Clare was able to manoeuvre things so that after Verity was taken care of, Simon and Emma were free to go to Nairobi alone.

'You can have my car,' she said to them. 'We drive on the left, as you already know, and your current licence is valid up to ninety days. Make for the New Stanley and their café, the Thorn Tree— it's a famous landmark in Kimathi Street. When you reach Nairobi from here, you go straight across Uhuru Highway, into Kenyatta Avenue, and that brings you to it.' She hastened, 'We're taking Verity for drinks with neighbours and, later, to the Nairobi National Park.' She laughed. 'You could really call it a suburb where the animals live!'

'Any lion?' Emma asked, on a note of excitement.

'Plenty. The main gate brings you into wooded Langata Corner, and you may well find lion strolling along the road there. You can see zebra, kongoni, gazelle, giraffe, impala!'

'I want to see the animals,' Verity said with enthusiasm. 'Perhaps we could all go together?'

It was left open and Emma said to Clare in the few seconds she had alone with her, 'Don't plan too obviously . . . Verity could resent it.'

Clare laughed. 'Trust me,' she said. 'One must start as one means to keep on, where Verity is concerned. We've been friends a long while, and I know her faults as well as she knows mine!'

'You're an incorrigible schemer,' Emma chuckled.

'Yes,' came the easy retort. 'Now off you go.'

Nairobi, the capital of Kenya, was a garden city, modern, cosmopolitan, with wide tree-lined streets where even the roundabouts were encircled by flowers, its avenues massed with magnificent bougainvillaeas. The suburbs, at varying times of the year, bright with flowering blue jacaranda trees. Semi-skyscrapers rose, white and dazzling, out of the surrounding Athi Plains.

Simon and Emma found the Thorn Tree easily, and having parked the car, walked a short distance from Kenyatta Avenue and turned into Kimathi Street. Here, safari firms met and picked up their passengers, while people gathered from all parts of the world. A huge acacia tree, with yellow bark, rose from the middle of the café, and the earlier tradition of leaving messages pinned to it still remained. Even though the old acacia had been replaced by a new one, 'Bill' still told 'Emily' that he'd 'meet her in London', and 'Rose' told 'Jo' that he couldn't 'see her in Amsterdam'! The world passed by—the atmosphere exhilarating, the sun casting deep shadows. The local population dressed in their colourful kitenge prints, or saris; businessmen in smart city suits, and well-groomed women in crisp cottons, suntanned and attractive.

Emma said, 'I feel that I'm standing aside watching myself sitting here, lazy, no surgery, and the warmth almost a way of life! December!' She looked at Simon and a little surge of pride silenced her. No one in sight could compete with his commanding presence, or challenge his powerful masculinity. He looked a man with whom no one would trifle; no one underrate. He might be disliked, but never ignored. He had the lean strength of the athlete and the dark smouldering passion of the lover, she thought, feeling again in imagination the vice-like grip of his arms, the demanding possessiveness of his kiss.

'An interesting reverie,' he commented. 'Where were you?'

She flushed.

'One must have secrets,' she said.

'And reasons,' he said on a note of gravity, 'that can never wholly be explained, or understood.' He changed the subject abruptly, 'I like your white dress with the red patterns on hem and neck.' He laughed. 'I'd not make a descriptive writer for a fashion magazine!'

'Thank you, all the same! There is one thing about coming to Nairobi in the winter: one can wear the clothes it hasn't been warm enough to wear in England in the summer! Sleeveless dresses have hardly been the thing—today, a bathing-suit would be ideal!' She stopped; the tension had vanished almost as though she and Simon had momentarily become two entirely different people as they sat there, looking into each other's eyes.

'I'm so glad you agreed to go to Mombasa.' He spoke reflectively.

'Did you imagine I might refuse?'

'I never take anything for granted, Emma.' His voice was low, almost enticing.

'Being taken for granted can *sometimes* seem comforting.'

'I disagree entirely.' There was suppressed anger in his voice; his dark eyes blazed as he added, 'It robs the individual of both pride and dignity.'

Emma's temper flared, the whole mood changing, emotion near the surface, 'Then this is where communication breaks down, making understanding impossible!'

'Meaning we're not talking the same language?' he demanded.

'Yes,' she cried, her head raised a few inches. 'We may be in the same country, but we're not in the same *world*.'

He drew her gaze to his with inescapable power, holding it in defiance. 'And if you believe *that*, you are lying to yourself,' he said fiercely, as unexpectedly his hand reached out and closed over hers in a hard, almost painful, grip.

His touch stemmed the flood of words, the inconsistencies. Passion drew them into a vortex, which they both recognised and mutely accepted.

Emma released herself from his hold and said with deliberation, 'Do you think Verity will object to our going to Mombasa—at the last minute?'

He was immediately defensive.

'Of course not. She realises that the heat, humidity and the journey would be too much for her. It is very kind of Clare to want to look after her, although, at the moment, that doesn't entail a great deal. You've spoilt her, of course—which she loves. It will do her good to be without you.'

'I *did* come to Hunter's Close to take care of her,' Emma reminded him.

'And to help me—which you've done expertly,' he said with a smile.

'You must give me a medal sometime!'

'Would you like to live here?' He shot the question at her irrelevantly.

'In the right circumstances—quite possibly.'

'What circumstances?'

'That's a loaded question.'

'It wouldn't be, to anyone else.' His voice was belligerent.

'I don't see why.'

'When a woman doesn't want either marriage, or any emotional involvement,' he suggested sardonically, 'she is shutting herself away from reality.'

'There is such a thing as taking words too literally,' she flashed, capitulating.

'Ah! Are we compromising at last?'

'Merely allowing for the inconsistencies of human nature.'

His eyes flashed, his voice was accusing, 'One either wants a thing, or one doesn't. You can't have it both ways.'

'Neither can you.' She threw the words at him.

A silence, deep, tense and unbearable, fell. All the warring elements gathered and petrified. Emma told herself that this was his opportunity to betray something of his feelings; even to explain why, since that fateful night, he had never made reference to the passion, rapture and fulfilment. Again, and this time bitterly, she smarted from the belief that it had been purely sexual on his part, and that, for him, there were no words needed to qualify the act. Yet there were times when she could swear that the memory of it lay between them in re-awakened ecstasy.

They sipped their coffee, watching Arabs, Asians and Europeans mingling with the African population, the kaleidoscope creating excitement and expectancy, the blue and gold of the day giving the scene a vitality that grey skies, rain and cold could never generate. The Swahili greetings of *Jambo*—Hello, heard frequently, as was *Asante*—Thank you, or *Kwa heri/Tutaonana*—Goodbye; see you soon; this, together with English, German, Dutch.

They left the Thorn Tree eventually and stood looking down Kenyatta Avenue—the broadest of the central streets, constructed in pioneer days, to enable twelve-span oxcarts to wheel around without difficulty. From there they walked through white-columned arcades, created as a protection not only from the rains, but the midday sun, and which sheltered the shops and restaurants along Mama Ngina Street. Eventually they drove to the vast Kenyatta Conference Centre in City Square, which dominated the skyline and had a revolving restaurant on top of a tower from which one could see Nairobi and the surrounding hills spread out in panoramic beauty.

'Infinity,' Emma said wonderingly, 'to remind man of his insignificance.' All was space, light, colour, the flowers massed—gigantic splashes of colour on an artist's palette—breaking up the view, giving life to inanimate buildings that shimmered and threw off reflected light.

They had spoken very little during their wanderings. Emma had bought a few things from various shops, finding it intriguing to have travelled over four thousand miles to hear her own language spoken as a matter of course—and impeccably spoken, too.

'You would like to go back?' Simon's gaze didn't linger in hers.

Emma, thinking he wished to do so, said quickly, 'Yes—please.'

She was hardly conscious of the short drive to Karen. A few perfunctory sentences were exchanged, and that was all. When the car stopped outside the house, she said politely, 'Thank you for taking me.'

'Thank you for coming.' His expression was inscrutable.

Emma hated the shattering change of mood, and went, dejected, into the shade of the hall, hearing the grandfather clock ticking with consoling normality. Anger, depression, would avail her nothing. She hurried upstairs to her room and stood looking out on the tranquil scene, the tall indigenous trees barely moving in the faint breeze; the flowering shrubs like brightly coloured stars, fragrant, exotic. And in the distance the Ngong Hills rose to a sheet of cloudless blue, clear, etched. For Emma, the sharp awareness of beauty around her seemed to bestow an extra sense, developed through the pain of loving and the need to be loved. Just then she heard footsteps coming up the polished staircase, and along the landing; heard Simon's door open and shut; its echo striking a mournful note in her heart.

No comment was made because of Simon's and Emma's early return, but Verity was delighted, and in the early evening they all went together to the Nairobi National Park to see the animals in the forty-four square miles of territory set aside for their habitation. The juxtaposition of wildlife in virtually a suburb of a thriving modern city was unique. There were signposted picnic places, but at the picnickers' own risk, otherwise one could drive along in the safety and comfort of one's own car and watch zebra, kongoni, gazelle, giraffe, occasional rhino, baboon, crocodile and hippo in the river pools, leopard, cheetah, hyena, warthog and ostrich.

The landscape was varied, with forest, hills, tree-less plains, and great expanses of meadow-land, rising impressively from the red earth.

'Lion,' Verity cried, 'walking over there!' She gave a little cry of delight. 'I know one can see them in the safari parks at home, but somehow, here, it all seems so different.'

'That's because,' Hugh said, 'the animals are in their rightful setting and can roam freely from Amsoseli and Tsavo right across the Athi and Kaputei Plains. They're only fenced off on one side of the Nairobi-Mombasa highway.'

Verity was sitting in the front of the car beside Hugh, while Simon, Emma and Clare had managed to squeeze in the back, so that they could all be together. Emma was acutely conscious of Simon's arm against hers, thrilled by the contact, even though it was a distraction. Several times he turned and looked straight into her eyes, defying her to ignore his presence. Their hands touched as they leaned forward to catch a last glimpse of a lion sauntering near a rockery. By the time they had reached the National Parks Office—and a beauti-fully laid-out Wildlife Centre by the main gate—she was afraid that he would be aware of her trembling limbs.

'This,' said Hugh, 'is an animal orphanage spon-sored by the Wildlife Fund.'

Clare added, 'It takes in abandoned and sick ani-mals from all over Kenya, rearing and, later, releas-ing the ones able to look after themselves. They also have an orphanage nursery where children can watch, and help with their feeding.'

'I've enjoyed it,' Verity said abruptly, 'but I'd like to go home. Watching strains my eyes, and the car's hot.' There was a querulous note in her voice, and she hastened, 'I'm getting selfish. I notice it, and don't like myself.'

'Don't worry,' Hugh said amiably, 'we'll get you home in no time.'

That evening Simon took Emma to dinner at the Norfolk Hotel, Verity being too tired to join them for a family outing.

'What I love here,' Emma said to Simon as they drove into Nairobi, 'is the evening darkness.'

'A tropical darkness,' he added, 'which seems full of light and deep purple.'

Emma shot him a swift glance.

'Romantic,' she said softly.

'Very.' He put out a hand and quickly clasped hers.

The Norfolk, in Harry Thuku Road, was part of Kenya's history and an 'old world' country-type hotel with every modern convenience. It built up from the Lord Delamare Terrace to the white-fronted balconies and half-timbered dormer windows, separated by a minaret-shaped turret, rising to the level of the roof tops.

The doorman, impressive and very tall, dressed in brown-gold trousers, long coat, peaked cap, was a cheerful welcoming figure. The reception area sustained the atmosphere, with exquisite flowers and African desk clerks in their dark suits, white shirts— their politeness striking. In the hotel gardens, *bandas*—cottages—suggested the intimacy of a country village and were a popular feature of the hotel. Simon and Emma finally ordered drinks on the terrace which faced the road. Moonlight mingled with the floodlighting, and flowering trees rustled imperceptibly in the faint warm breeze.

'This,' said Emma, 'is perfect.'

'The beginning,' Simon said significantly.

The steward, in his green apron, black trousers, white shirt and black necktie, served them with their ice-cold martinis. They did not speak as they raised their respective glasses, but looked into each other's eyes, and passion mounted, quickening her heart-beat, making her hands shake so that she was forced to lower her glass to the table, anxious to conceal her emotion. Her voice was unsteady as she said, 'I'd like to be staying in one of the cottages—with a veranda overlooking the gardens——' She stopped, the implication of her words obvious.

'I can think of nothing I'd like more,' he agreed, his voice deep, almost caressing.

A few minutes later they went into the dining room—large, flower-decked; even the square pillars had wall vases filled with carnations. The stewards in their long trousers, white shirts, red jackets and black bow-ties, looked resplendent, their movements swift, yet unhurried, and with that incredible silence which is a part of the African heritage.

Emma looked around her, noticing the large table in the centre of the room, from which curry was served—the guests helping themselves.

'I love curry,' she said, 'but not tonight.'

Simon ordered burgundy, saving, as he explained, the champagne for Mombasa.

They selected melon, entrecôte, finishing with

fruit salad served from a scooped-out fresh pineapple which, with the top of the fruit replaced, made a novel decoration.

And all the time they talked, Emma felt that she was listening to an orchestra playing before the curtain went up on an unknown play.

A page walked through the room holding a board, with a tinkling bell on a stick, the name of the guest required written for all to see.

'That's an original idea,' Emma exclaimed, avidly interested in all that was going on around her.

'What would you like to do tomorrow?' Simon asked a little later, when they were having coffee in the lounge with its painted white walls, and highly-polished marble floor.

'I'd like to laze in the garden with Verity, Hugh and Clare. Verity would enjoy that, too.'

'You've been very kind to her—*very* kind, Emma.'

Emma was to remember those words; at the moment she glowed in his appreciation.

Before leaving the Norfolk they were drawn to its aviaries, where many species of Kenyan birds were housed. Birds of all colours, their brilliance incredible. The red and yellow barbet, with white spots; ross turaco, having an orange-yellow face and bill, crimson flight feathers and crest; violet-backed starling, with bright violet-blue upper parts and throat, white belly, and yellow eyes—every species a riot of vivid colour.

'But that long-tailed widow bird!' Emma cried. 'Jet black with bright red and buff shoulders.'

'Its tail two foot, or more,' Simon said, reading the description. He stopped abruptly, adding with total irrelevance, 'You said you would like to fly around the world . . . I believe you meant it.'

'Of course,' she said firmly. 'One day, I shall.'

His voice held an almost sad solemnity, 'I'm sure you will.'

The words hung between them; it was as though, with the reference to her going round the world, emotion died and numbness replaced excitement. There was silence without anger on the return journey to Karen.

When they parted that night, Simon leaned forward and kissed her gently on the forehead.

'I hope life fulfills all your expectations, Emma,' he said, his voice grave and subdued, as he turned and went swiftly into his room.

CHAPTER NINE

EMMA experienced an almost self-conscious nervousness as she faced Simon at breakfast on the morning of their trip to Mombasa.

'You must have dinner one night at the Tamarind,' Hugh said. 'It's on the Nyali side of the creek, looking towards the old harbour. The sea food there is superb. And they provide red bibs for messy eaters!'

Emma laughed. 'Any dummies, too?'

'And, today, have a break at Tsavo Inn for a drink and sandwich. It's about half-way between here and Nyali.'

Verity was still in bed when they said good-bye.

She drew a hand across her eyes and looked a little wistful.

'Enjoy yourselves,' she said.

'I haven't a coat,' Emma cried as they reached the front door.

Clare laughed. 'You never need a coat here—a cardigan sometimes or, in the rains, a raincoat! It will be well into the eighties where you're going, and you'll feel much hotter because of the humidity.'

'Nurses,' Simon exclaimed, 'think of everything.'

'And doctors *forget* everything,' Emma retorted with a smile.

'That's true enough,' he admitted, as they went out to the car.

'Mombasa, here we come!' Simon said a short while later as, out of Nairobi, they headed for the coast.

Emma felt the relief in his voice, the sudden easing of tension. 'Must be the doctor in me,' he added. 'I never believe I am going anywhere until I'm actually on the way!'

'Always that emergency.'

'Yes.'

Neither voiced the fear they had shared lest, at the last minute, Verity might not be well.

Stretches of shrub, barren tracks, dotted with huge cacti and powdered with red dust, made Emma say, 'This could be Wild-West country. You almost expect to see a film-star appearing, gun in hand!'

The vastness of it all, however, brought a feeling of awe. The skyscape was panoramic, the blue deepening as the miles were annihilated, and they came nearer and nearer the coast. It was hot, even with the car windows wide open, and while the road was tarmac, the light was dazzling and tiring.

'Would you like me to drive for a bit?' Emma asked.

'No;' he said immediately, 'I like you sitting there, beside me. At least this is *one* part of the world to which *I* can take you!'

She longed to tell him that he could, if he wished, take her anywhere at any time! Instead, she said, 'We're going to enjoy this, Simon.'

'Is that a prediction?' He shot her an inquiring look.

'Yes.' She crossed her bare arms and stroked them. 'We shall be able to swim in the Indian Ocean! I've only just realised that. It sounds exotic!'

And at last they came to an avenue of coco palms on the outskirts of Mombasa, the atmosphere amazingly different. Colourful Arab shops, their wares all out on the pavement; the smell of spices, the fascinating Eastern influence in juxtaposition with modernity. The Arab population in their flowing robes; the Indian women in black, eyes veiled and in purdah. Narrow streets, balconied houses hung with merchandise, rather like bunting, giving a festive air; then, as they left the native quarter, they reached the tree-lined Moi Avenue, which was dominated by giant white sheet-metal elephant tusks, which formed an archway overhead.

'The gateway to East Africa,' Simon said.

A short while later they crossed the comparatively new dual-carriageway bridge which took them to Nyali. The harbour scintillated in the sun. Ships of all types, and all nations, lay at anchor while Arab dhows whispered of forgotten history, and red fishing boats reflected their bright colour in the vivid blue water.

Nyali Beach Hotel gleamed white and imposing as it nestled amid luxuriant tropical gardens and, through a frieze of coconut-laden palms, looked out across the coral sea.

The heat was terrific, but as they went into the air-conditioned reception hall, the change of temperature hit them as though they had walked into a refrigerator. But once they became acclimatised, it offered a perfect atmosphere. The sense of space, of light; the gleaming polished floors and, as always, the masses of flowers which were part of the decor, rather than merely a decoration.

Emma felt a thrill of pride as she stood with Simon at the reception desk and they signed the register, the staff welcoming and courteous.

Their adjacent rooms were large, each with its own bath, veranda and sea views.

'Would you like to rest?' Simon asked, as he stood in the doorway, the baggage already taken care of by an Arab porter, who moved like a shadow, unobtrusive, efficient.

'I think I'm drugged by the beauty of it all,' she replied. 'I'd like to unpack and feel that I'm *here*.'

'I'll give you a knock in about half an hour,' he suggested.

And as they stood there, they were both aware of the fact that they were alone, on holiday. It gave their relationship a new and dangerous dimension.

Later, they lazed, and wandered around the hotel grounds, with a palm-fringed swimming pool, wide beaches and silvery-white powder-like sand. Just before changing for dinner they decided to have a swim. The water was crystal clear and almost sapphire. Emma, in a bikini, stood slim, yet voluptuous, her figure perfect, with the long curve from breast to waist emphasising her slenderness. She felt Simon's appraising gaze upon her and noticed his strong fine body—broad shouldered, narrow-hipped. He reached out and took her hand as they ran and plunged into the warm ocean. Only a few other couples were in distant sight, for here there were no overcrowded beaches, the expanse was too vast—an illimitable stretch, curving gently, a fringe of tall rustling palms rising above sky and sea, cutting into the horizon.

In that moment Emma was happy. There were no problems; no tensions, just the joy of swimming with Simon beside her.

'This is magnificent,' he cried, as he darted away and then cut back through the almost imperceptible waves.

They swam, and afterwards lay sensuously close on the soft sand. He turned and his arm reached out and came to rest across her shoulders, his hand lowering to her breast and cupping it, at first with gentleness, and then with passion. She tensed, but did not draw away. She knew he could feel her heart pounding, and abandoned herself to the thrill of his touch as it crept to caress her bare flesh in the moment that his lips found hers in a convulsive ecstasy.

Then, suddenly, abruptly, he drew away and got swiftly to his feet. Emma, quivering with emotion, knew that the moment had been too dangerous to prolong.

They parted and met again in her room, sitting on the veranda and having a drink from the minibar provided. Neither wanted to break the spell of the harmony that lay between them in the memory of desire.

Twilight came with the suddenness that turned the sky into a screen of rainbows, and then sprayed fire over the blue that piled great rifts of colour—flame, orange, rose—its reflection dyeing the sea, so that the one was an extension of the other. The palm-fringed beaches were suffused by an uncanny roseate glow that looked as though a magician's wand had dusted them with rubies. And as the sun went down in glory, so the moon rose, clear and golden, tinting little islands of cloud a soft purple that turned day into night in a final majestic tranquillity. The silence was that of the tropics—mysterious, unearthly, drawing them into it with a magical power of its own.

They went down to dinner like two people treading on moonbeams, bewitched by the beauty of it all and by each other.

The champagne Simon had ordered awaited them at their table in its ice-bucket.

'To dine in a room overlooking the Indian Ocean,' Emma said, 'has a fascination that's indescribable. And I love the red decor, and the little candle in the centre of the table.' She stopped, the word *love* suddenly, almost poignantly, important. If only Simon would utter it; if only a few words would accompany passion and desire. Or his lips tell her what, on occasion, his eyes seemed to say.

After dinner they explored the grounds, danced in the open air, passion like a third presence between them as desire mounted. Floodlighting vied with the moon to give the scene an unearthly radiance as they wandered on to the beach, where Simon drew her into his arms, almost savagely, as though he would defy the world in order to possess her. Every nerve was sensitised as his hand traced the outline of her body, touching her breast in a moment of rapture. She ached for him to take her there, amid the sanctuary of the palm trees, moonlight pouring down upon them; yet she was bitterly conscious that, once again, this was no more than his expression of sexual need, not of love which would have given purpose to her surrender. His lips were hard against her own, his arms vice-like, until, almost as though reading her thoughts, they fell to his side while he looked down into her eyes, seeking, but not revealing, as he moved a pace or two away, leaving an emptiness within her that was pain.

Pride enabled her to ignore the fundamental issue and make light of the intimacy.

'A tropical night plays strange tricks,' she murmured a trifle breathlessly.

For a second he reached out, his arm around her waist, his lips seeking the warmth of her mouth, as he held her suffocatingly close.

'I'm going to take you to your room,' he said in a hoarse whisper.

'No.' It was a cry. 'I'd rather go alone.' And before he could speak, she was running across the beach, heart thumping, emotion tearing at her, ecstasy lingering, his touch still weakening her. And she knew he was standing watching, and not moving in pursuit.

Morning brought a degree of normality and they set off to see the city. Looking at him, Emma cursed herself because she couldn't accept him merely as a lover, using these days to satiate desire without thought of tomorrow.

If only she hadn't fallen in love with him. Love imposed restrictions; narrowed the possibilities unless given, and enjoyed, with complete abandon.

Mombasa was like nothing that Emma had imagined. On the one hand it was a thriving bustling city, proud of its tradition; its prosperity based on Kilindini Harbour; on the other, the old town, lying between Makadare Road and the old harbour, was a fascinating example of cosmopolitan hustle, with a multitude of languages. Its narrow streets were dark eerie tunnels, overshadowed by tall houses with elaborately carved ornamental balconies.

'The kind of places one has only seen in films,' Emma said as they drove through the shadowy streets. Itinerant Arabs were selling from traditional long-beaked copper pots, and oriental music drifted out from the shops—mostly owned by Asians— moneylenders, goldsmiths, tailors. Oriental mosques and temples, the Jain Temple being an impressive symbol of the prosperous Indian community.

'It looks like a gigantic iced wedding cake,' Emma exclaimed, 'those domes and the intricate patterns on the pillars above them.'

They drove and walked intermittently. At

Mombasa's old port, they watched dhows which still carried goods to the Gulf. The atmosphere seemed to hold a breath of history, the shops overflowing with merchandise displayed in organised chaos, their amiable owners smiling broadly and not for one moment expecting to receive the price they asked. And over it all hung the sweet smell of spices. Arab chests, brasswork, carvings, silks, jewellery—all were offered with much gesticulating, until Emma was too confused to know what she wanted—if anything. Finally, they went into Yusuf Jaffer's perfume shop. Exotically-named scents lined the walls. Since they were made without alcohol, they did not evaporate, consequently lasting a considerable time. Simon bought her an expensive-looking bottle saying, 'Not to be worn during surgery!'

The heat lay upon them—heavy, thick, airless. Dark alleyways were no more than shadows where children played, darting about like the lizards to which Emma had become accustomed. Modernity and crumbling age; pure Arabs in their beaded hats and embroidered cloth gowns; the Hindus, the Swahili men who wore long white robes, or, more often, a brightly printed length of cloth wrapped around their waists like a skirt, and called a *kikoi*. The women in *kangas* wound beneath their arm-pits—mid-calf length. Europeans, sight-seeing, like themselves, now becoming exhausted as the noon-day sun approached. The light almost hurtful because of its brightness; the sky low, cloudless, and vividly blue.

'Mad dogs and Englishmen,' Simon said as they returned to their parked car. The seats as they got in, were like hot coal.

'They told me at the hotel that the Oceanic would be good for lunch,' he said.

'Let us go back to Nyali,' Emma pleaded. 'Shade; a cool drink.' She laughed. 'We shall stick to these seats!'

'Have you enjoyed being a tourist?' He smiled at her indulgently.

'Very much. Contact with the orient, perhaps; and the fact that it has all been in existence for so long.'

'Some historians talk of Mombasa dating back to 500 B.C.'

'That's about how old I feel at this moment—so *hot*,' Emma laughed.

'My fault, for allowing you to be out at this hour.'

'It's only *just* midday!'

They drove back to Nyali. Emma changed into a sun-suit and Simon into shorts.

'Do you think I should telephone Karen?' he said as they sat by the pool, sipping their long iced drinks.

Emma was immediately alert. 'Why?'

'Courtesy to Clare, quite apart from anything else.'

'Clare promised she would ring us should anything go wrong.'

'I suppose I cannot quite believe in this freedom.' He hastened, 'From work—everything.'

'Are you quite sure you're enjoying it?' she asked deliberately.

'Quite sure. Isn't that obvious?'

'Nothing is obvious with you, Simon.'

'Words,' he countered, 'are cheap. Better too

few, than too many.'

'That depends on the circumstances in which they are uttered; and their sincerity.' She looked at him challengingly.

He lowered his gaze and sighed.

'That's an over-simplification,' he murmured, 'and it's too hot to argue.' The smile he suddenly turned upon her was disarming, and she couldn't combat it with anger. Coudn't he understand that because she had slept in his arms, she was more vulnerable? And sensitive to the situation? She realised that he would not force his attentions, or pursue her should she run away. Had she not been a participant, she would have accepted it as a highly intriguing situation. As it was, how could she ache for his love and yet now withhold the ultimate expression of it? How long before she betrayed her feelings?

And when, that night, they reached the Tamarind she caught at her breath because of its romantic beauty. Near the old bridge, it stood out white in the moonlight, in Arab style, with a large carved oak door. It seemed to lie like a pearl against the sapphire velvet of the night. Its wide arches and key-patterned roof completed an unforgettable picture. And as they were shown to their table on the terrace overlooking the creek, Emma cried, 'Everything is so unexpected, somehow . . . the lights opposite . . .' She gave a little exclamation of delight.

'Fort Jesus gleaming over there,' Simon pointed out. He paused, looking at Emma whose eyes were starry with appreciation, her taut young figure outlined in her beautifully fitted lilac-shaded dress, her red lips parted so that he said in a breath, 'You look enchanting, my darling.'

My darling. No music had ever sounded more beautiful, or touched her so deeply. She remembered the night he had first called her that.

His features were etched in the violet darkness, the power of his attraction overwhelming. Her hand fluttered out to meet his, clinging in a spasm of yearning. And it seemed in that moment that all the words had been said.

They ate delicious sea food, exotically served, as they watched the lights across the creek twinkling and spearing the dark waters with liquid gold. The warm air touched them sensuously.

They lingered long after the meal was over, savouring their brandy, until Simon said, looking at her intently, 'Shall we go?'

She nodded. The night still lay ahead, full of promise. He had never seemed closer, or been more attentive. They drove back to Nyali through the tropical darkness, their silence the measure of their emotion.

A reception clerk said, as they went to the desk to collect their keys, 'Dr Conway, there's been an urgent telephone call for you. Will you ring Karen.'

Life seemed to drain from Emma as she heard the words, and she and Simon hurried to his room to ring Clare.

Verity's good leg had given way as she was going down the veranda steps and she'd had a nasty fall; her ankle was wrenched. In addition, her sight had deteriorated to a point where she could hardly see— the two misfortunes following one upon the other.

'There's nothing for it, Emma,' Simon said dully,

as he replaced the receiver, 'we must go back tonight. The responsibility is far too great for Hugh and Clare to shoulder—quite apart from Mother's point of view.'

'Of course,' Emma agreed. 'Obviously I heard what you said . . . I'll go and pack.' And with that she hurried from the room.

The journey back to Karen was an anti-climax which plunged Emma into an empty, almost hostile, world. A blind might have come down between her and Simon who sat beside her, tense, his expression inscrutable. She was thankful when they finally turned into the drive of Mitha Lodge. It was five o'clock in the morning, but both Hugh and Clare were up and Ricky appeared to attend to their baggage, having elected to be on duty.

'I'm so *sorry*,' Clare said in greeting, looking from face to face. 'I hated having to ring you.'

'It was the only thing to do,' Hugh added, 'for Verity's sake.' He did not betray the fact that Verity had demanded Simon be called back.

Verity put out her hand gropingly and then clung to Simon as he moved to the side of her bed.

'Thank God you're back . . . never leave me again. *Please.*' She went on, choked, 'I'm frightened. Now I can't stand, and I can't see out of my left eye; and the other one is all misty. My feet tingle and my right hand is numb and useless.' An hysterical note crept into her voice. 'I want to go home—*home*. Hugh and Clare are wonderful, but you must get me home.'

'Not before Christmas,' Simon said adamantly.

'Oh, yes—yes! Doctors can arrange things. I

ought not to have come here . . . I feel *safe* at home.'
Tears gushed to her eyes. 'They don't need to know
that I *want* to go—you can say that I must see a
specialist—anything.'

Simon took her pulse and examined the ankle
which Clare had bandaged.

'Tell me about the fall.'

'I was going down the veranda steps when my
good leg gave way.' She did not confide that Clare
had warned her not to attempt the steps alone. 'You
will take me home,' she persisted.

'What about Emma? Her holiday?' His voice was
gentle, but firm.

'Emma won't mind going back. She has Stephen,
don't forget. Anyway, we can't plan our life around
her, and if she doesn't want to return with us, then
we shall have to get another nurse . . . I'm *helpless*,'
she finished on a note of panic, shrinking back in the
bed. 'I want to go home,' she cried again, like a
child. '*Simon*, did you *hear* me?'

'Yes,' he replied, his voice weary. 'I'll get a flight
on the 28th. You have Emma here to look after
you.'

'I don't like the heat and the light and the polished
floors—it's all *different*.'

'The 28th,' Simon said with finality, and patted
her hand. He knew that to prolong their stay after
then would not be in anyone's interest.

'And you'll tell them that *you* think it right for me
to go home?'

'Yes.'

'You sound tired.'

'I *am* tired,' he admitted.

'I want Emma,' she said suddenly, sharply.

'I'll send her to you, but don't forget she will need some sleep today.'

He spoke to Emma that evening after they had both snatched a short rest.

'This isn't just a question of returning home,' he began. 'Mother will need general nursing now; she'll be in a wheel-chair and have to be got into it and out of it. Her dependence will be infinitely greater, and your work infinitely harder. The thing is, are you prepared to cut short your holiday and continue the nursing?' He paused and looked at her solemnly. 'I told you I didn't take anything for granted, Emma, and I'm not doing so now. But I must *know*.'

Emma realised that this was a crisis and that her future, her happiness, was at stake. If she stayed on, she was plunging more deeply into danger; tying herself to an invalid in order to remain in the same house with the man she loved. As against that, she could remain with her parents for a while, and then take a job anywhere in the world. Travel. Nursing was, after all, the Open Sesame.

'There is another point,' Simon pointed out, 'you will not be able to do very much, if anything, in the practice. I'm aware that my partners will have something to say about that—particularly Stephen.' He regretted the words the moment they were uttered.

Emma said coldly, 'We are not discussing Stephen.' And as she spoke, the voice of reason whispered that if the moonlit nights at Nyali had not inspired any avowal of love from Simon, what else could possibly do so? 'I take it,' she added, 'that Verity wishes to return home immediately after Christmas, even though I can look after her here.'

'Now that she is partially blind, wouldn't it be very strange if she did not cling to her own home?' He studied Emma with sombre reflection. 'I'm waiting for your answer to my question.'

Emma felt fury building up; fury because she could not walk away from him, and the words were involuntarily torn from her, 'I'll return with you, and nurse Verity.'

'Thank you.'

Was it possible, she asked herself, that they were the same two people who had sat on the terrace of the Tamarind? The man who had called her, '*My darling*'?

CHAPTER TEN

To Emma the following days were like years, since that bitterly cold grey morning when they left the warmth of Kenya and returned to Hunter's Close. Parting from her parents had been emotional. The Christmas festivities were by no means over, and the house was bright with decorations and fairy lights. A well of depression seemed to be drawing her down into its murky gloom as she looked over the winter scene at Winchcombe, the trees bare, dripping with rain, and mists blotting out the Cotswolds.

'*And you are Emma*'. Simon's first words to her

echoed fancifully as she looked at him over the
breakfast table on that January morning. He was
eating mechanically, and suddenly said, 'We haven't
had a chance really to talk since we got back, Emma.
There's been so much confusion, and you've needed
ten pairs of hands.' His expression was considerate,
his voice gentle.

'It will be easier when Verity can handle her
wheel-chair with more confidence. I can't leave her
for more than a minute or two.'

'Her frustration is part of the trouble ... I've a
committee meeting at the hospital this evening,' he
went on swiftly, 'perhaps we could have a drink together when I get back.'

'I'd like that and I shall be here,' she said, con-
veying that he need have no worry on Verity's account.

He put aside his table napkin and got to his feet.
'Yes, thank God,' he murmured. He paused, and for
a second the silence seemed alive with the unspoken
thoughts that lay between them, then, almost as
though not daring to trust himself, he went swiftly
from the room.

Odile, coming in from the garden, witnessed, with
shock, the exchange of glances, aware of the unmistakable evidence of love in Emma's eyes.

'How's the patient this morning?' she asked
lightly.

'So-so.'

'There's no way of knowing what other symptoms
may develop,' Odile reflected, 'but with these re-
current episodes, remissions are far less likely ... I
think you're a saint to look after her as you do.'

'I'm a *nurse*,' Emma exclaimed, 'and one feels so *sorry*.'

'She can be very difficult.' Odile was watching Emma carefully as she spoke.

'So can we all!'

'It's pretty grim for Simon—although he'd never admit it.' Odile sighed and added, with faint cynicism, 'I had a bet with myself that you'd be home before the month was up. Oh, I know about the fall and all the rest of it, but even had Verity been as well as possible, the result would have been the same.'

Emma said quietly, 'It doesn't really matter—does it?'

'Suppose you're right . . . . Ah, well! Must dash. They'll be banging on the doors otherwise!'

Emma stared after her, puzzled by some indefinable resentment in her attitude and manner.

Verity was in a truculent mood that day, and no matter what Emma tried to do to placate her, she was rebuffed. Brett and Stephen looked in to see her, receiving some caustic comments about her electric wheel-chair, and how she would have preferred a manual one, if only she had the strength in her hands and arms to use it.

'Is there any chance of your getting out tomorrow evening?' Stephen asked Emma as he stood in the doorway on his way out, Brett having a few final words with Verity.

'I can't promise anything,' Emma said.

'And you can't be tied here, day in and day out, either,' Stephen said aggressively. 'I've hardly seen anything of you since you got back . . . Emma, please

try to understand. I want to *talk* to you. I shall have
a word with Simon about your being imposed on,
and——'

'You'll do no such thing,' she cut in. 'No one is
twisting my arm, Stephen. I'll have dinner with you
just as soon as it can be arranged.'

'Can I rely on that?'

'Yes.'

'If only you'd marry me,' he said under his breath,
'and come away from all this.'

Emma looked at him, knowing his worth and
genuinely fond of him. Impatience stabbed her because one word from Simon meant more than all the
avowals of love from anyone else.

'Until tomorrow,' Stephen said, raising his voice
as Brett joined him, and he and Brett went from the
room together.

'I haven't seen Odile today,' Verity complained,
aggrieved. '*Seen!*' she repeated in ridicule. 'People
are only shapes now. A house full of doctors and all
they can do is give me vitamin pills, or whatever it is
they call them . . .. There's a play I want to listen to
on the radio tonight . . . but I get sick of the radio.'
She spoke in a flat monotonous voice, one sentence
merging into the other without expression. There
was a little, rather pathetic, pause before she added,
'You're so good to me, Emma; so patient. I wish I
weren't so bad-tempered sometimes, but I get very
weary of it all . . . I don't know what I'd do without
you and Simon,' she finished forlornly.

Emma touched her hand in a little affectionate
gesture, murmured a few soothing words, and then
hurried to the telephone as it rang, taking the call in

the hall just as Odile appeared. It was from Mrs Morris, frantic because she had tried to put on an elastic stocking, got it twisted, and could neither get it on, nor off, and it was tightening on her painful leg. As she lived alone, and had no one to help her, could someone come to the rescue?

'Emergency?' Odile asked.

Emma explained, adding, 'The patient doesn't usually wear a stocking, but a bandage. But this is her second thrombosis attack, and pressure on that leg is dangerous.'

'Wouldn't take you a minute.'

'I can't leave Verity.'

'Good heavens, *I'll* stay with her; she won't even know you've gone. And Simon shouldn't be long, either.'

Emma nodded, half-talking to herself, 'It's his patient, and she only lives a short way from here . . . you're sure you don't mind?' She was thinking of the drink Simon had suggested.

'I played nurse long before you came,' Odile said significantly. 'Better hurry.'

Verity sat very still in that silent room. Perhaps, she thought hopefully, there would be more remissions; perhaps she would be able to see again, at least enough to distinguish the roses when they bloomed. Why did everything seem so hushed, as though the world had died? Where was Emma? Where *was* she? The radio, that was it. She wanted the radio . . . what time was it? Had she dozed? She called, 'Emma!', panic exploding in that grey world where very little light penetrated. Anxiously, she swung her chair round in the direction of where she believed the radio to be, lost her balance and hurtled towards the fireplace ...

Simon, having left the committee meeting earlier than he had hoped, came into the drawing room to see Verity lying inert, blood oozing from a head wound.

'Oh, my God!' he cried as he rushed to her side, calling, 'Emma! Jessop!'

Verity stirred, concussed, confused. 'Home ... want ... to go ... home. Emma ... left me.'

Jessop appeared, stunned by what he saw.

'Where's Nurse?' Simon asked, then, 'Help me to get my mother to her room.'

'I haven't seen Nurse,' Jessop answered, shaken.

Verity was lying on her bed when Emma returned a matter of seconds later; a nasty purple-red lump was visible on the side of her forehead.

'Where have you been?' Simon demanded.

Emma, looking shocked and bewildered, replied, 'To help Mrs Morris with her stocking – what's happened?'

'Fetch Odile,' Simon said, 'I can't believe that you'd go out and leave my mother alone.'

Odile's voice reached them, calling out smoothly, 'Where *is* everybody?' She appeared on the threshold, gasping and appalled as she saw Verity.

Emma said immediately, 'Odile——', but the rest of the sentence froze on her lips as she realised that Odile had no intention of telling the truth.

Verity mumbled, 'Emma? Why ... leave ... me?'

Odile said, 'Oh, dear! So you left her alone. You

must have known that it was dangerous. Now it will be a question of withstanding the shock, in her condition—her powers of recovery.' Odile was so concerned, so convincing.

Simon moved from the bed to allow Odile to reach her patient. His voice held anger, anxiety and disbelief as he exclaimed, 'Unfortunately, Emma was more concerned about Mrs Morris.'

Emma stood there, numbed, her world collapsing about her. Any kind of explanation would, she knew, be useless in the face of Odile's attitude and silence.

Verity was found to have extensive bruising of ribs and shoulder, abrasions on one leg and mild concussion.

The house took to itself a hushed misery, depression and fear. People moved quietly; even the telephone bell seemed like an alarm. Emma kept vigil as though Verity were a beloved child. Only once was she able to speak to Odile alone, and then she asked brokenly, 'Why didn't you stay as you promised? You *knew* I would never have left Verity, had you not offered. What have I ever done to you that you should——?'

Odile cut in darkly, 'I don't know what you're talking about. You are the nurse; it was your job to look after your patient, not mine.' With that she walked away.

On the second night Emma said despairingly to Simon, 'Verity's breathing is bad——'

His eyes met hers in sad contemplation.

'If only you'd been concerned earlier . . . now it is rather late.'

After he left her, Emma prayed, uttering the words

aloud, 'Please God, don't let Verity die . . . don't let her *die*.'

But Verity developed terminal bronchial pneumonia, her heavy stertorous breathing the last desperate sign that the battle was lost. She died four days after the accident.

And because she had always needed so much care and attention, the impact of her death was the more devastating.

'The coroner will have to be notified,' Simon said dully, 'since death followed an accident.' He might have been talking to himself, but the partners and Emma were present, shocked by the swiftness of events. No mention had been made by Simon, or Odile, of Emma's alleged neglect in leaving Verity alone. Simon squared his shoulders, 'We must carry on as normally as possible.'

Stephen studied Emma, whose face was ashen. Now that her patient was dead, would she still stay at Hunter's Close? The prospect of her leaving agonized him.

Simon mentioned this to Emma a little later in the day.

'I'd rather you remain until after the funeral,' he said stiffly.

'It would be unthinkable not to do so,' she replied shakily. So! There was no question in his mind of her remaining on any permanent basis. And, again, tormentingly, she knew that no man could compromise when it came to the loss of his own mother. And from his point of view she had precipitated Verity's death.

'I don't want conjecture, or gossip, to surround

my mother's accident. This is a doctor's house, and events can be exaggerated out of all proportion.'

Sympathy for him welled within her; there was hurt in the sadness of his eyes; a strange melancholy about him, and when he looked at her, he seemed to be questioning, watchful. She burst out involuntarily, 'Oh, Simon, I'm so sorry; so desperately *sorry*.' Her voice broke.

He misunderstood the reason for her words and said, 'No words of mine could possibly condemn you as much as, I am sure, you condemn yourself.'

'But——' she began, and sighed—a deep heavy sigh.

They lapsed into silence.

Odile sought him out that evening in his study.

'You don't have to talk,' she said softly. 'I understand. It's all so tragic and—and unnecessary. I suppose that is what makes it harder to bear . . .. Don't worry, Simon; just let *us* look after the practice. Everyone has been so kind.'

He nodded.

She sat down for a few minutes and then got to her feet.

'You'd rather be alone . . . I just wanted you to know that I was around if needed.'

'Thank you, Odile . . .. It's all so sudden; so many *changes*.' He looked stricken.

She glanced back at him as she reached the door.

'Try not to think of the future, the changes . . .. Of course we shall have to replace Emma, but someone will come along. Why not take a sedative, and get a good night's sleep?'

After Odile had gone, he remained sitting there,

stunned, bereaved, and consumed with anger and disillusionment.

Emma fastened the last of her cases and stood looking out over the familiar grounds, and at the sun-drenched countryside beyond. What had begun as almost an idyll, was now ending as a tragedy. She could not make it less. Her estrangement from Simon was like losing a limb, or worse; and to leave without the comfort even of his friendship seemed unendurable. Throughout the intervening days he had maintained a polite silence, addressing her only in front of other people, as at the funeral, and ignoring her presence in the practice.

'I shall not be seeing you again,' Emma said on her last morning as Simon was about to leave the breakfast table. 'I've just a few things to collect from my office, and that's all.' She tried to keep her voice from shaking, and to avoid looking at him for more than a second at a time.

'Where are you going?' It was the first personal remark he had uttered since Verity's death.

'To friends in London, and then back to Nairobi.'

'I see.'

'You don't, Simon, and you never will ... goodbye.' She could not offer trite, stilted words, when her heart seemed to be choking her, and sobs were rising in her throat.

'Goodbye, Emma,' he said almost curtly.

Neither looked back as they moved in opposite directions. But Emma hurried to her room, great sobs tearing at her, tears running down her cheeks, the ache in her heart like an illness. She felt physically sick, her body hollow and merely a vehicle for pain. She was leaving Hunter's Close and would never again feel the touch of Simon's lips, or his arms around her; never know how much, or how little, she had meant to him. She caught sight of her tear-stained face and sat down at her dressing-table, drawing on courage and fortitude as she repaired the make-up to which she had resorted. No one must know how she felt, and at least she had the sadness of Verity's death to account for any display of emotion when she finally said goodbye to the staff. She got to her feet and walked purposefully to the door. No one should fault her courage on this occasion, least of all Odile.

Her office was empty and silent. The faint clicking of Rose's typewriter; the voice of Mrs Hedley on the telephone, were part of that silence. Maude came into the room saying, 'I thought I heard you.'

'Just collecting my personal things.'

'We all wish you weren't going.' Maude looked solemn. 'Everything seems miserable and foreign. It's all so sad.'

'Yes,' Emma murmured, 'that is the right word.'

She went into the main office and said her farewells. Gloom seemed to have settled on the practice, and eyes looked into eyes, half-questioningly, because they were not really sure even of the right questions.

Brett shook Emma's hand, his grip painful, saying gruffly, 'Won't seem the same without you.'

And all the time Emma was listening for the sound of Simon's voice. Was he in his consulting room? Would she catch a glimpse of him? She both longed to do so, and yet dreaded the prospect.

Stephen insisted that she had by no means seen the last of him, reminding her that he still had infinite patience and perseverence. Odile joined them, quiet, controlled. 'We shall miss you, Emma. Good luck.'

Emma didn't speak; she couldn't. Simon's door stood ajar as she reached the corridor, but no sound came from within the room. A wave of sick disappointment washed over her, and then, suddenly, unexpectedly, his voice rang out, sharp, commanding, 'Emma! Odile! I want to speak to you both.'

He appeared, having seen his last patient out, and paused for a second before taking up a position at his consulting room door, waiting for them to precede him.

Odile cried, flustered, 'I've my visits——'

'This won't take long.'

Emma murmured that she was about to leave.

He might not have heard her as he shut the door. There was a second of tense, almost electric silence, before he began, 'I've a message for both of you from Mrs Morris.'

Emma's voice was cold, almost cutting, 'I've nothing to add about my visit to Mrs Morris.'

Odile sighed, irritated.

'She means nothing to me except that she is a patient.' Something in Simon's expression, his whole demeanour, made her add breathlessly, 'Simon, what is it?'

'This,' he almost thundered. 'Mrs Morris was very upset to hear, just now, that Emma was leaving, and asked me to thank her again for coming to her rescue that night.' He paused, and added, 'She also said that she was grateful to Dr Craig for *taking over* to enable Emma to get away.' Fury blazed in his eyes. 'It was you, Odile, not Emma, who left my mother alone, and you were cowardly enough to let Emma be blamed for it.' His voice was like a whiplash.

With a groan, Odile's words tumbled out. 'God forgive me; I must have been mad.' She added with a despairing cry, 'But I swear I didn't know anything about her fall.'

Simon looked at Emma. 'What can I say to you that wouldn't seem like an insult in the circumstances? But why—*why* didn't you tell me?' His voice was low and appealing.

'Because even had I tried, you wouldn't have believed me, and would have condemned me more for implicating Odile; and I didn't mention Verity to Mrs Morris. And I could hardly involve a patient in my defence—that would have earned your contempt.'

He sighed, contrite, and shook his head. 'I'm afraid that's true. The enormity of it all, from my point of view, was that it was my *mother*, and you seemed morally responsible for her *death*.'

Odile sat down and hid her face in her hands.

Emma asked sorrowfully, 'Why, Odile? *Why?* We were *friends*.'

Odile, pathetic, beaten, murmured, 'Something snapped, and some murderous jealousy possessed me.' She gave a little shiver of distaste. 'I've never done anything like it before in my life. I wanted to cause you trouble; to discredit you.' Her voice rose and then dropped almost to a whisper as she confessed, 'I'd loved Simon for so long—so long.' In that moment her pride vanished. 'And even though it was never mentioned . . . you knew, Simon, didn't you?'

'Yes,' he said, hushed.

'And after you arrived,' Odile went on, looking at Emma with wide eyes, 'he gradually stopped coming to the cottage. God knows his visits were innocent enough. I owe you both the truth, and you cannot despise me more than I despise myself.'

Simon gave a deep sigh.

'*Odile!*' he murmured, anger sliding into compassion.

'I've caused so much misery,' Odile went on regretfully, 'and but for Mrs Morris . . . ironical, isn't it? I never even thought of her.' She looked at Simon. 'May I speak to Emma alone? There are things I'd like to explain.'

Simon left them and Odile rushed on, 'You see, I thought I could be big and noble; I thought I could bear the prospect of Simon loving you, but it was when I knew that *you* loved *him* something snapped, and I couldn't bear it.'

Emma gasped, 'But, how——?'

'It was in your eyes that morning when I came into the dining room and I felt it was my doom. Without you, I believed I had a chance, but with you, loving him, you had everything on your side, and I seemed to have nothing. But, oh *Emma*, I'm so sorry . . . I'm not really like that. I'll never forgive myself, or stop feeling guilty, but, dear God, I didn't dream that I'd be indirectly responsible for Verity's death.' Tears ran unchecked down her cheeks as she spoke, her utter dejection and misery making Emma say gently, 'I bear you no grudge, Odile. Jealousy——' The word died away.

'And I didn't like your loving him. I was jealous even of *that*. I dreamed dreams and made others pay for them. And I've hurt myself most in the end.' Her voice broke, 'I loved him so desperately, and Simon's not a man you can forget—or fight against . . . but you know all about that.'

Emma said quietly, 'Thank you for not mentioning my feelings just now.'

There was a little unhappy silence before Odile said, 'I'm so *sorry* . . . Oh, Emma, forgive me one day, if you can.' Her sigh was deep and distressed. 'Now it is I who will leave, and you who will stay.'

'My staying is by no means certain,' Emma exclaimed, the relief, the thankfulness, fading. 'I know nothing of Simon's feelings.'

Odile made no comment, just got to her feet and seemed to drag her body from the chair as though every movement had become an effort. 'Thank you,' she murmured, tears welling into her eyes again; 'thank you for the friendship I betrayed.' And with those words she went swiftly from the room.

Simon returned almost immediately, drawing Emma's gaze to his with all the passion and desire that had been an integral part of their relationship.

'I thought I had lost you,' he cried. '*Lost* you; and it was hell.' His voice became low and pleading, 'Do you think you could bear to stay now?'

'Only if it is forever,' she murmured. 'Only if I'm

sure of your feelings for me.' And even as she spoke, his presence weakened her, emotion flaring between them as their hunger for each other mounted.

He reached out masterfully and drew her into his arms.

'I love you—deeply, passionately. I've want to tell you for so *long*.'

'Then why, oh *why* didn't you do so?'

'Because I felt it wasn't fair to tie you,' he said quietly. 'I knew I ought not to have made love to you, but I wanted you so desperately without realising that I loved you, too. And afterwards, it worried me because I wondered if you despised me and regretted it. That's why I didn't risk introducing any talk of love. But I counted on your loving me enough to give me some indication . . . but you ran away, and that angered me, as well as making me love you all the more!' He drew in his breath sharply as he looked down into her eyes. 'Do you love me, my darling?'

'Yes,' she said tremulously. 'I knew that night . . .'

His lips went down on hers, the thrill of passion newly found; his arms tightened around her with a possessiveness that robbed her of breath, and as he drew back he asked a little fiercely, 'Why, if you loved me, did you run away—on the beach at Nyali, particularly?'

'Because I wanted so much more than I thought you had to give, or *wanted* to give.'

'What fools we can be when we're in love!' he cried with an exulted little laugh, and then changed his tone as he said, 'I also had a responsibility, which I felt it would be unfair to ask you to share. Mother's condition could not permanently improve and I freely admit that I hadn't the courage to ask you to marry me, or the strength of will to let you go . . . I had neither courage, nor will-power, when it came to you. I couldn't resist you.'

'I'm so *glad*,' she whispered. 'Never even *try* to resist me!'

'But,' he said with a sudden solemnity, 'I had made up my mind to tell you that night after we'd been to the Tamarind. I knew I couldn't go on being with you, hiding behind curtness, or indifference. I argued that you could only refuse to marry me . . . and then——'

'What would you have done?'

'Asked you again,' he said purposefully.

'I like that idea. . . I must resist you!'

'At your peril.'

'And that makes it completely *ir*resistible . . . 'Oh, Simon! Are we really here like this? Or shall I be back in that horror even of an hour ago?'

He sighed; a deep sigh of satisfaction. 'I told Odile I was in love with you,' he confessed. 'I thought it was only fair. I'm so grateful she didn't mention the fact, because this moment wouldn't have been quite the same . . .. Can you forgive me for all my stupidities?'

'I love you,' she said simply.

'My *darling*.' His lips parted hers again as desire swept over them, and it might have been a starlit night in the tropics, so great was the passion that held them.

And as they realised that there was work to be done, Emma pleaded, 'Be gentle with Odile.'

'*You* can say that?'

'We don't want any shadows,' she said softly, adding, 'I'm sure Verity would agree.'

'Yes,' Simon agreed, 'I believe she would.'

'And, Simon?'

'Yes?' He tilted her chin and looked into her eyes.

'I must be able to read the signposts; to know where I'm going.'

'Would the church in Winchcombe be the right direction?' he asked tensely.

'The perfect direction.' And with those words she went back into his arms.

'Everyone loves romance at Christmas'

The Mills & Boon Christmas Gift Pack is available from October 9th in the U.K. It contains four new paperback Romances from four favourite authors, in an attractive presentation case:

The Silken Cage	– Rebecca Stratton
Egyptian Honeymoon	– Elizabeth Ashton
Dangerous	– Charlotte Lamb
Freedom to Love	– Carole Mortimer

You do not pay any extra for the pack – so put it on your Christmas shopping list now.
On sale where you buy paperbacks, £3.00 (U.K. net).

Look out for these three great Doctor Nurse Romances coming next month

THE DOCTOR'S DECISION
by Elizabeth Petty

When Staff-Nurse Anna Forster meets the new Senior Surgical Registrar at the Calderbury Royal she realises that most clouds *do* have a silver lining. It is love at first sight for Anna, but is it the same for Paul Keslar?

A BRIDE FOR THE SURGEON
by Hazel Fielding

By marrying Pip, Hallam Fielding would gain a clinic nurse, a general secretary, cook, housekeeper and slave – and all for free! Even if he could never love her, was it sufficient if she could somehow make him want her?

NURSE RHONA'S ROMANCE
by Anne Vinton

Rhona was disappointed, though not heartbroken, when her romance with Chris Willson came to nothing: all the same, she was glad to have her work as a district nurse to take her mind off things. And she was even more thankful for her career when her next romance, with Dr Alex Denham, crashed to disaster.

On sale where you buy Mills & Boon romances.

The Mills & Boon rose is the rose of romance

<u>Two</u> more Doctor Nurse Romances to look out for this month

Mills & Boon Doctor Nurse Romances are proving very popular indeed. Stories range wide throughout the world of medicine – from high-technology modern hospitals to the lonely life of a nurse in a small rural community.
These are the other two titles for October.

BRIGHT CRYSTALS
by Lilian Darcy
In the French Alps Nurse Natalie Perroux meets a handsome member of the ski rescue team – and they are instantly attracted. What she doesn't foresee is the heart-rending tangle which follows the unexpected arrival of an old boyfriend from England . . .

NIGHT OF THE MOONFLOWER
by Anne Vinton
After a year's parting, physiotherapist Deborah Wyndham is at last on her way to Nigeria to join her fiancé John. But that special something seems to have gone out of their relationship, and kindly interference from the attractive Jean-Marc Roland makes things even more complicated . . .

On sale where you buy Mills & Boon romances

The Mills & Boon rose is the rose of romance

One of the best things in life is ... FREE

We're sure you have enjoyed this Mills & Boon romance. So we'd like you to know about the other titles we offer. A world of variety in romance. From the best authors in the world of romance.

The Mills & Boon Reader Service Catalogue lists all the romances that are currently in stock. So if there are any titles that you cannot obtain or have missed in the past, you can get the romances you want DELIVERED DIRECT to your home.

The Reader Service Catalogue is free. Simply send the coupon – or drop us a line asking for the catalogue.

Post to: Mills & Boon Reader Service, P.O. Box 236, Thornton Road, Croydon, Surrey CR9 3RU, England.
*Please note: READERS IN SOUTH AFRICA please write to: Mills & Boon Ltd., P.O. Box 1872, Johannesburg 2000, S. Africa.

Mills & Boon
the rose of romance